# [Façade]

## By

First Edition

ISBN: 979-8-9934210-2-5

# Marcus: The Millionaire

The problem with me wasn't running my luxury transportation business; it was being Marcus Vance. My office wasn't just an office; it was a glass cage overlooking the entire Uptown Charlotte skyline, a testament to the Prime Executive Transport empire I'd built with nothing but pure tactical nerve and very long nights.

I had mastered logistics, yes, but more importantly, I had mastered the performance of success. Everything in life is a performance; you can either be the star of it or the extra.

I tossed a worn basketball, the same one I had played with since college, from one hand to the other, barely looking up as my Head of Operations rattled off quarterly revenue numbers. The fleet of obsidian-black sedans and SUVs was my fortress, symbolizing the distance I kept from the world's chaos.

I was the architect of perfect order, providing seamless travel for clients who viewed the rest of humanity as traffic or something to navigate.

But in that high-gloss, pressurized world, honesty was the highest-risk commodity. Every woman I met, every networking partner, saw the empire I had built first. The success became a filter, making the pursuit of anything real feel like a carefully coordinated gain that I couldn't seem to get right. I don't know if it was my fear of being used, so I self-sabotage, or are women just looking for security without substance?

"The fleet is immaculate, the margins are strong, but the CEO is restless," I finally admitted to the empty room after my manager left. I grabbed my keys. I hadn't driven a client in years, not since the days when Prime was just two cars, red bull, and a prayer.

***

"Cleverness is a burden, Marcus. Who wants to walk around being the smartest person in the room all the time?" Lee drawled later that week, casting his lure into the glassy water of Lake Travis. Lee, ever the comedian, was right, but not in the way he thought. Cleverness wasn't a burden because it was hard; it was a burden because it was isolating.

"You only say that because it allows me to out-maneuver you on the court and at the negotiation table," I replied, leaning back in my camp chair. I didn't bother correcting Lee; letting people underestimate my effort while overestimating my inherent talent was part of my strategy.

Gary, ever the quiet observer, chuckled. "He's got you there, Lee. But Marcus, both of y'all are trash on the court. How about you apply some of that cleverness to catching some fish? Or, when are you going to apply that cleverness to something that actually challenges you? Like, say, dating a woman who isn't mainly interested in your portfolio?"

"Damn, Gary, I thought I was the sarcastic and funny one. I see I am starting to rub off on you." They laughed.

The question hung in the humid air, heavy with unspoken truth. My penthouse apartment with its skyline view felt colder than the back of my own sedan. I owned the entire city's privatized transportation infrastructure, yet I couldn't find a genuine connection in any of its million squares of glass and steel.

"Why are you fools worrying about my love life? You two are in no position to give me any relationship advice." That was the best I had at the moment.

"And yet, you still ask for it," Lee countered.

"All we are saying is you've got to put that brain power to good use. Besides, the dating pool is crazy right now. No matter what bracket you are in. You see what I am going through with my situation," Gary added.

"Gary, you slept with your baby mom's sister for crying out loud. You deserve whatever situation you are in." Lee said, laughing hysterically.

"I was drunk, it was dark, it was her twin sister, and I didn't know two grown women were playing these little kid games. Toya was out doing her thing with another man, and her sister tried to cover for her. I didn't know she was going to throw it back like that or try to say I came on to her when she was in our bed naked." Gary explained.

"Calm down, man, we believe you. You are starting to sweat and scare the fish off." Lee and I looked at each other and started laughing.

***

We decided to head out to the cigar lounge for some drinks. A new spot opened up on Tryon that we want to try out. We called ahead and had a section ready for us.

The place had a nice vibe. It had a different feel compared to the grass walls and lamb chops that every other place seems to have.

I was wearing a nice black dress shirt and black pants, and I threw on my Jacquard evening jacket. It was not fancy, but it was a head-turner. My waves were spinning, and my beard was moisturized. I finished the look with my Stefano Ricci leather shoes and a couple of sprays of Tom Ford's Black Lacquer. Oh yeah, I was going to leave with something, well, that was the plan.

We all sat down at the booth. Looking at the three of us together, one might think we wouldn't hang out, but these two are my day ones. Lee was wearing his NY fitted cap, a black-and-red graphic tee, black jeans, and some black-and-red Jordans. Usually, someone wouldn't get inside wearing his outfit, but he knows everyone and spends money, so he gets us into a lot of spots.

Gary, on the other hand, looks like your everyday senior-level executive—Polos, slacks, and dress shoes. Gary was the lead accountant for a pharmaceutical company, and Lee was a producer who worked with some of the most prominent artists.

"Do you even know what type of woman you want?" Gary asked as he took a puff of his cigar.

"I really don't have a type. I want to meet someone that I can talk to, trust, and not have to worry about her being after my money." I answered as I took a drink.

"I believe that falls under trust, my guy. And why are you still drinking Crown and Coke like you are not rich? That's probably why you can't keep a woman." Lee said as he sipped on his henny.

"Man, you are drinking Hennessy, you can't talk about anyone," I snapped back.

"I can talk about all that damn cologne you sprayed. What the hell are you trying to cover up?" Lee teased.

"I'm not going to lie, it is a lot, though. Made my eyes water a little," Gary said as they busted out laughing.

"Y'all got all the jokes tonight," I said, laughing along with them.

"On the real, you can't go wrong with anyone else you try to talk to because Mia was crazy as hell, and I don't think you will find anyone as crazy as her," Gary said as Lee raised his glass to the statement. We continued the night talking, drinking, and strategizing our next money move as three black successful men who made it out of our situations.

"Hey, handsome." Two women walked up to us who looked like they had turned twenty-one yesterday. Wearing see-through clothing and looking like they were on a mission.

"You just had to open your mouth, G," Lee said as he took another sip.

"What can we do for you ladies?" I asked

"Oh, we liked that. You tell me, handsome, what can you do for me?" I looked at Gary and Lee, and both of them had their cups to their mouths, looking at me. I could almost see their smile through the mugs.

"You ladies are more than welcome to join us."

"Okay, that's cool." The girl in the red dress said. I got up so she could sit between Gary and me. Lee did the same for the woman in the black dress. The conversation wasn't too bad, but there was a clear difference. The girl in the red dress set her phone on the table. The phone lit up, and I noticed two young kids in the photo.

"Are those your kids?" I asked right away. I was not too interested because of the age gap, but the two kids were a deal-breaker for me. There is nothing wrong with kids, but I want my own, and it's okay to have that preference.

"Yes, those are my babies. They are really smart and don't get into trouble at all," she said it as if she was trying to pitch a project. Just then, someone slammed their hand on the bar loud as hell, and it caught all of our attention for a minute.

"Alright, ladies and gents. I am going to call it a night. Here is my card if you ladies need a ride in the future or tonight." I gave them both cards and paid for their drinks.

"How about tonight?" Red dress said to me.

"I have an early day tomorrow, so I will pass for tonight, but get home safe." I gave the boys the wrap it up signal and called my driver.

# Zahra: The Perfectionist

The courtroom was my natural habitat: a place defined by strict rules, sharp logic, and zero tolerance for deviation. I was lethal in litigation, capable of finding the single, fatal flaw in a fifty-page contract faster than anyone in my firm. My life was defined by precision and controlled excellence.

Yet, when I wasn't in court, the precision blurred.

I started as an intern right after college and helped the company out of a deal that never should have been made. They instantly gave me a permanent position. Eight years later, I made partner. Everything in my professional life was perfect. My love life, on the other hand, was ready to take a plea deal.

"I swear, Al, they treat dating like another merger," I sighed, swirling the cabernet in my glass as I lounged on Alicia's plush velvet sofa. "They analyze the assets, calculate the return on investments on a second date, and then, if they're pleased with the valuation, they try to acquire me for a late-night hook-up." Which is a hell no for me.

Alicia, a public relations wizard who knew how to market sincerity even if she couldn't find it, gave me a sympathetic glance. "It's the environment. You're attracting the hyper-optimized executive clones. They're great on paper, dreadful in bed, and they have the emotional depth of a corporate bylaws amendment."

"Exactly! I want someone who doesn't see me as another conquest or another line item on his five-year plan. I want the honest guy, the one who takes pride in a hard day's work and... laughs easily." The yearning in my voice felt dangerously close to desperation. Oh my God, am I desperate.

Alicia leaned in, a conspiratorial glint in her eyes. "You need a palate cleanser. Someone completely outside the system. Maybe a brilliant, brooding artist or a handsome park ranger." She suggested. "You keep dating these lawyer types and keep getting the same results. Try something new. Or someone new. Using the rose is fine and all, but nothing compares to being bent over, hair snatched, and pussy stretched." She looked off in the distance as if she were reliving the event.

"Earth to Alicia," I laughed, a genuine, less brittle sound this time. "A park ranger who understands the nuances of a Securities and Exchange Commission violation? Unlikely. I need someone authentic, Al. And apparently, authentic doesn't shop in my tax bracket."

"Well, they can shop in my brackets all night if he acts right." Alicia stepped out of the bathroom looking like she was ready for anything. Her curls were short and bouncy, down to her shoulders. She had minimal makeup on that made her beautiful face and skin pop. We were both brown skinned. I was a little shorter than she was.

She had on this black dress that came down halfway between her knees and ass. It hugged her body like it was trying to stay warm on a cold night. Her long legs showed flawless skin, and her ass was the perfect shape. Round and plump. Those five days a week are paying off.

She wore open-toe heels that showed off her pretty feet and fresh pedi.

"You know what I think your problem is? You dress like you are going to court all the time. I mean, who still wears the whole three-piece pajama set to bed?" I looked at what I had on.

I had on a beige checkered three-piece suit with closed-toe heels. My dreads reached my back, but I sometimes put them up in a bun at work to look more professional. I shouldn't have to. See, I did it again, everything goes back to work. Maybe I'm stopping myself from experiencing something real.

"Are you okay, girl? You are doing that thing again where it looks like you are talking to yourself, and I be wanting to put you out every time you do it." I looked up at Alicia and busted out laughing.

"Girl, let's go," I ordered a ride as we left her apartment. We were going to this new cigar lounge that just opened up on Tryon.

***

We got out of the Prime Transport and had to show our IDs at the door. It feels good to be older and still have to get checked at the door. Inside the lounge was beautiful, and there was not a grass wall in sight. I looked around and didn't see anyone who stood out. We were walking to the bar when I saw a table with three guys and two women who appeared to be barely legal. Some men are disgusting.

We sat down at the bar and ordered our drinks. "This place is nice," Alicia said in her, I'm drunk already tone. She has always been a lightweight. One time in college... Well, I will save that for another story.

"It really has a nice vibe, and the drinks are amazing," I added as we toasted to a good weekend and took a sip.

"How are you two ladies doing tonight?" We heard a voice from behind us. Two gentlemen were standing there looking at us like we were a snack, like we were something to be devoured, and if the tall one keeps licking his lips like that, I am going to take them for a test ride.

"We are fine, as hell," Alicia said, starting to get really giggly, like she always does when she drinks.

"Yes, you are. We were wondering if we could buy you two ladies a drink and have a conversation?" The tall one asked. He was clearly lusting after Alicia, who was clearly buzzed.

I looked at the quiet one and said, "Is he going to talk for you all night, or are you going to try to get some pussy?"

"See, I told you this was a waste of time coming over here to talk to her bougie ass," the shorter guy cried out.

"So you can talk, I see. Bartender, I will pay for their drinks since he wants to act like a little boy, and they can be on their way."

"Girl, chill, I'm trying to get stretched."

"No, I'll pay," the shorter guy says as he takes a fifty out and slams it on the bar. "Here is another for therapy." He slams another fifty on the bar.

"Bro, chill, you're acting mad weird," tall, dark, and handsome tried to intervene, but I was ready to match his energy.

"Here is a hundred to help fund your sex change," I slammed a hundred-dollar bill on the bar hard enough to make some heads look our way.

"I think it's time for you to leave," the bartender told the two men hovering over us. They walked off in utter defeat, and I kept my Benjamin.

"Girl, you are crazy as hell," Alicia said with a laugh.

"I am over tonight, girl. That really blew me. Let me know when you make it home." I called my transport and went outside to get some fresh air. As I was waiting, I saw this man get into the back of a big, all-black SUV. He was too far away to get a good look at his face, but he had on way too much cologne. Well, at least it smelled good.

# Marcus: On Sight

Wednesdays are my busiest days. Appointments, meetings, marketing, and a lot of the boring, essential things I have to do to keep everything running smoothly. I keep a company car in case I have a VIP client or need to get to a meeting without a driver available.

A call came in about an hour before our VIP pickup. A last-minute family emergency had taken the primary driver out of the rotation for that particular trip. One of my managers tried to find someone to fill the spot, but was unsuccessful, and he was currently on a transport.

I, already on edge from a dull afternoon of board meetings, grabbed my phone off my desk and went to work. I looked at the manifest: a high-profile public relations firm's client was heading to a major philanthropic gala. I was also invited to the event, but I didn't feel like going.

"Fine," I muttered. A rare moment of necessity, a chance to escape the glass cage and remember the feel of the road. I grabbed the keys to a fresh, obsidian-black sedan—a vehicle I knew intimately, having chosen every bolt and stitch—and slipped into the charcoal suit, the unofficial uniform of my carefully organized empire.

I pulled up to the stately brick building on time, adjusting my cufflink. When I stepped out to open the door, I was Marcus Vance, owner, disguised as Marcus Vance, driver.

Then, she appeared. She wasn't just beautiful; she was the physical embodiment of the competence and sharp brilliance I admired in a woman, wrapped in a black suit that looked molded by willpower, confidence, and sexy all at once.

The air around me grew dense, and for the first time in months, my quick, clever mind went utterly, entirely blank.

"Are you going to open the door, or do I need to call an Uber?" Her voice was so perfect. Soft but stern. The ideal voice for the narration of your favorite book. I wonder what her moans would sound like.

"Sorry. Good evening, ma'am. Marcus, Prime Executive Transport. Ready when you are."

"Where is Jay?"

"He had a family emergency to go to."

"That's nice, so he is having the baby today," she informed me, which was weird because this was the first time I had heard about it. She got into the back seat.

"Did Jay tell you which manager was giving him a hard time?" I asked to get more information about it.

"No, but he did call him a fat ass. Are you going to tell the manager or something?"

"No ma'am. I will report the manager to the owner, because mediocracy cannot be tolerated in this company."

"You sound like the boss, or do you just love your job?"

"No ma'am. I am just a driver, and yes, I love making sure you get to where you are going safe and sound."

"If you are going to flirt with me, you should probably stop calling me ma'am."

"Well, it would be inappropriate for me to keep calling you beautiful."

"Oh wow! You are really working on those stars."

"Amongst other things."

"Really? So tell me…"

"Marcus. My Name is Marcus."

"So, tell me, Marcus, what other things are you working on?"

"The same thing we all are. Financial freedom, generational wealth, and creating opportunities for others to reach their full potential." She gave me this look like she was really thinking about something. "Is everything okay, beautiful?"

"Zahra, my name is Zahra." We made eye contact in the rear-view window. I can tell she was flustered, so I played it cool the rest of the trip.

The ride was a blur of contained laughter and accidental intimacy. The car's small space became a theater for our chemistry, as if we were mixing the right chemicals for something explosive to take shape.

She spoke about the ridiculousness of corporate event fashion; I offered quick, dry wit about the traffic patterns. Her smiles were dazzling, genuine, and utterly distracting. I hadn't felt this alive talking to anyone in years. I felt the pure thrill of being judged only by my conversation, humor, and presence—not by my portfolio. It was addictive.

When we arrived at the dazzling venue, the moment seemed to stretch. I, ever quick on the draw, leaned in slightly.

"For the record, a woman this interesting shouldn't be left to the whims of corporate schedules. Could I have your number and show you the city through my eyes?"

Her smile softened, tinged with genuine regret. She reached into her clutch and pulled out a slim business card case—not to hand me hers, but to take mine.

"I appreciate that, Marcus. But you seem like a genuinely good guy, and I'll be honest," she paused, her eyes challenging me. "You're probably out of my league."

She slipped the card into her clutch and disappeared into the flashing lights of the party. I stood there, the rejection smarting, but the sheer thrill of her having taken the card eclipsing the sting. Out of her league? I owned the entire damn league. I grinned, already planning my next move.

I spent the next three days like a hunter obsessed. I tagged the client company in the dispatch system for every single run they booked, regardless of the time or destination. I suffered through dull trips to the airport and long waits outside boring boardrooms, all for the fleeting chance of seeing that sharp, beautiful face again.

# Marcus: The Confession

The following afternoon, I found Gary and Lee already set up by the water, the sun glinting off the bobbers. I skipped the fishing and went straight for the camp chair.

"You look like you just lost a million-dollar contract, which, knowing you, means you probably earned three," Gary commented, not looking away from his line.

"Worse. I met someone," I admitted, running a hand over my stubble. "I drove her a few days ago. She was flawless, Gary. A corporate lawyer, sharp as glass, and she didn't look through me. She saw Marcus, the driver, and she laughed at my jokes, and we made this intimate eye contact like we both realized something at the same time."

Lee sat up, eyes wide. "Wait, you met a woman who didn't immediately google your net worth? That's gold, Marcus. A real keeper." It's hard to tell when he is being genuine or playing around.

"It was," I said, the memory still tingling. "She was talking to me about traffic, and logistics, and ambition, and she didn't know that I was the guy who owned the logistics. It was the most honest conversation I've had in years. I felt like the actual me was enough."

Gary finally glanced over; his expression was serious. "So, what's the issue? You close the deal?"

"She told me I was out of her league nicely," I sighed, the words tasting bitter. "She said I seemed like a genuinely good guy, but she's out of my league. She thinks she's too high-class for the driver. She took my business card, but she wouldn't give me her number."

Lee started laughing, that signature goofy roar of his. "This is the most incredible, backward ass thing I've ever heard! One of the richest men in the city is getting rejected for being too poor!"

"I know it's ridiculous," I snapped, then calmed myself. "But that's why I can't tell her. I won her over as the driver. If I tell her who I am now, it invalidates the entire interaction. I want the honest relationship, and the only way to get it is through this ridiculous, beautiful, frustrating facade."

"I don't know, man, this definitely feels like it can go south in a terrible way," Lee said as he cast his line into the lake.

"I know, but if I tell her who I really am, how would I know it's me that she likes and not just what I can do for her?"

"You are a smart man; I am sure you will figure it out. It really must be lonely at the top. Now stop crying, you are scaring the fish away."

Gary shook his head slowly. "Let me get this straight, you are just going to gamble the first woman you actually want on a lie? It's a high-risk strategy, even for you."

I looked out at the water, the moment having passed. "High-risk, but necessary. I had my shot. I was the driver. She said no. I'll probably never see her again."

"I agree, she probably hasn't thought about your ass since you dropped her off," Lee added as something was on his line. He hooked it and started to reel it in.

"Do you ever have something positive to say?" I asked, slightly annoyed at his comments.

"I caught this fish!" Lee held up a catfish weighing about 6 pounds. I laughed and shook my head. These two are my day ones.

# Zahra: The Post-Mortem

I kicked off my heels the moment I stepped into my luxury skyrise apartment; the silence after the gala felt huge. I picked up my phone to call Alicia, knowing I needed to download the whole ridiculous, devastating encounter immediately.

"He was perfect, Al," I whispered, pacing while I waited for her to answer. "Tall, impeccable manners, the kind of quick, dry wit that just doesn't exist in our corporate bubble. He was just... good. And he made me laugh until my stomach hurt." I held my stomach as if the joyful ache was still there.

"A handsome driver? Sounds like a plot device, not a date," Alicia said dryly through the phone speaker. "But you liked him. So, you flirted, you gave him your card, and now you're going to get his number, right?"

"No," I admitted, stopping by the window. I looked out at the city, my city, the city I fought for every day. "I took his business card, but when he asked for my number, I told him no. I...pretty much told him he was probably out of my league." A cloud of guilt and shame fell over me.

The line went silent, then Alicia let out a gasp. "Wait, you told him that? Zahra, you're a corporate lawyer who just won a major antitrust case. He's driving a car. What are you talking about? Where is the lie? You are above that girl. I am sure there is a fine ass executive that hasn't lost his mind somewhere out there. A driver, though?"

"Exactly. He's driving a car. He's clearly working hard, he's ambitious, but he's a driver, Al. Court schedules, million-dollar settlements, and networking events define my life. I can't fall for a man whose life is about traffic patterns and tips. It's not fair to him, and it's certainly not practical for me." My defense sounded tight, lawyerly, and entirely miserable.

"But... you also rejected the one genuine, funny man you've met in five years that checked most of your boxes because he earns an honest living?"

"I rejected the impracticality, Al! I don't want to date someone who will always feel small in my world, or someone I'll have to lift up constantly. I wanted the honest guy, and I found him, but the honesty came with a job description that just doesn't fit mine." I rubbed my temples, the logic overwhelming the yearning. "I couldn't risk it. I couldn't risk liking him that much and then watching it all fail because of a gap we can't bridge."

"You did say he had big ambitions and seemed like he was going to make things work out for himself, isn't that enough?"

"Potential and ambition are not enough anymore; not in these times."

"So, the only man who is worthwhile is the finished product? There is no room for anything else?"

"Whose side are you on, Al? It's really not sounding like mine right now."

"Z, all I am saying is that I understand both sides of what you are feeling. He's a driver, and you are a lawyer. He has ambitions, but he is not where you would like him to be."

"Exactly!"

"Exactly my ass! What has dating men in your "bubble" given you besides some nice dates and horrible dick?" I hate that she is my friend sometimes.

"Just because you are sleeping with my doorman doesn't mean I should lower my standards."

"First of all, Chris and I just fuck and that's it. There are no late-night conversations or dates, just in and out. Secondly, I am not out looking for something everlasting like you are. That ship sailed a long time ago. Lastly, we are up late in the evening talking about a man that you claim is out of your league. Are you okay?" I really hate that she is my friend now.

"Damn, tell me how you really feel, Al."

Alicia sighed, a long, frustrated sound. "Z, you are a master of self-sabotage."

"I know," I confessed, the tightness finally breaking. "But he was so genuinely charming, and I want everything about him. But I did the right thing. It was one amazing conversation, and it's over now. I'll never see him again."

"Girl, get off my line with all that dramatic shit. Chris just got here. You will be okay, Z."

"Okay girl, love you, and have a great night." I hung up the phone and laid down thinking about Marcus. Like, could this really work? Going through the pros and cons in my head was not that hard. I had all real pros, a few made-up cons, but only one real con.

I looked at the time and it was almost one o'clock. This man has been in my head for hours. I noticed my body getting really sensitive. My nipples were hard, my thighs touching felt erogenous, and my clit was begging for some attention. I reached for my drawer and pulled out a flower toy with a suction feature.

While on my back, I spread my legs. The hum of the toy was too familiar. My pussy was already wet from just thinking about this man. What is he doing to me? The suction on my clit felt different this time; it felt more intense, more real than usual.

The sensation pulled at every nerve in my body, and I let it. I closed my eyes and pictured his smile and lips. Like I can look down and see his nice waves breaking on the shores of my warm, wet beach. Every crash of his tongue sends a jolt through my body. Each suction pulls me deeper into my ocean. I moan softly as my tide begins to rise.

The pleasure takes control over me as my back arches, and my toes retreat closer to my feet. My free hand caresses my thighs, my stomach, my breast, as if it has a mind of its own. My hair raised with every thought of his smile. Chills went through my body when I thought about his eyes. My whole body wanted this man except my brain.

There was no lifeguard on duty, and I was about to drown in my own waters. Each moan louder than the last as I rocked my hips to the rhythm of my motion. I could feel his hands grip my thighs and pull me into his mouth. His tongue made laps around my clit.

I moaned louder; the gaps in between them were closing. I squeezed my breasts hard like the pain would bring me out of this trance, but it only sent me deeper. I moaned as my hips rocked up and down.

There it was —the biggest wave I had ever seen was coming. I wasn't afraid; I wanted it to hit me with all of its force. I grabbed the sheets and braced for impact. I moaned louder and louder until it hit. The climax traveled from every part of me.

I tried to hold it in, but I couldn't. I let out a continuous moan as my body exploded in pleasure and release. I dropped my toy and used my hands to strum my clit until the squirting stopped, until the moaning stopped, until my breath slowed, and I just lay there, a survivor of my own waters, stranded in loneliness.

# Zahra: Boomerang

It's been a week and some change since I last saw Marcus. I was beginning to think that day was all a dream. There was no time to dwell; I had to get my team ready for court.

My assistant booked the car for the pre-trial hearing, and as I reviewed the driver manifest—a habit I developed just in case—I saw the name Marcus show up, but nothing. The company he worked for was picking us up, so maybe I'd get to see him again. I need to focus.

A sudden, potent rush of adrenaline hit me, the kind that usually precedes a major cross-examination. I put myself on the docket instantly, determined to play this out.

The black SUV pulled up. Sam was already outside waiting. When the car stopped, Sam opened the door for us to get in. On court days, we request that the privacy window be up so I can't see who is driving us today.

When I sat in the back seat with my two colleagues, Sam and Chloe, we started talking about the case. I made sure my focus was entirely on the brief. We were talking animatedly about a closing argument when the screen came down.

"There is an accident ahead, I will have to detour from the planned route, but I will still have you all there early." The driver said. The heat rose in my body as we made eye contact through the mirror. Almost two weeks later, and my body is still activated by him; it was Marcus.

I was trying to ignore the fact that the driver was the most beautiful and interesting man I had ever told "no" to. I managed to go almost five minutes without looking up, discussing legal precedent like my life depended on it. He kept the window cracked on purpose. I could feel his eyes on me. If my colleagues were not here, I would give this man a show he would never forget. What am I doing, focus Zahra.

Then, out of pure habit, my eyes flickered to the rearview mirror. There he was. Marcus. The playful, too-intense gaze of my driver met mine—just for a fraction of a second—before he smoothly refocused on the road. But that one look was a bomb going off in the pristine silence of the luxury SUV.

"And counsel will object to that on the grounds of... are you even listening to me, Zahra?" I stopped, realizing my colleague had to repeat himself twice. The blood rushed to my cheeks and somewhere else as well. I glanced up again, catching Marcus's eye in the mirror; he gave me the faintest, most controlled smirk. I felt a familiar rush of heat and a sudden, catastrophic loss of professional composure.

"Zahra, you seem distracted," Chloe pressed, her voice laced with professional concern. "Is everything okay?"

"I'm sorry, what were you saying about the precedent?" I asked, forcing myself to look down at the fifty-page brief, but the words swam. Every single thing I was saying felt like a stage whisper in a tiny theater where only he was the audience. The air conditioning was humming, the leather seats smelled faintly of expensive cleaner, and the low, rhythmic hum of the engine was the soundtrack to a decision I hadn't made yet.

I had to force my thoughts back to unlawful acts and statutes intentionally, but every time I did, I could feel the invisible thread of his amusement tugging at my focus.

The distance between the front and back seat felt like an electric current, tight and ready to snap. I even imagined him smiling into the mirror when Sam started talking about a particularly dull contractual clause.

When we arrived at the courthouse, the city's chaos seemed to intensify. Sam, ever the gentleman, efficiently opened the rear door for me. I was gathering my files, mentally preparing the first line of my opening statement, when I looked up and saw the charcoal suit, the familiar height, and the face of the man who had just occupied every corner of my mind for the last twenty minutes.

Marcus was standing right there, holding the door open, his eyes full of that quiet, knowing challenge. He wasn't just a driver; he was an event, perfectly orchestrated. The shock was intense. For a corporate lawyer who lives and dies by preparation, this moment of genuine, high-stakes surprise was intoxicating. My opening statement was forgotten.

I took the opening statement I was about to give and stuffed it back into my briefcase. Instead of rushing out, I told my team to go on ahead—a clear signal that the urgent business was no longer the case. I walked back to the driver's window, the sharp scent of expensive perfume and determination preceding me.

I leaned in close, my voice low and steady. "I was wrong to say what I said before, and I am done analyzing the assets. I'm free tonight, if you are."

Marcus met my gaze, his smile slow and genuine. "I've been free for days, Zahra. Just waiting for your closing statement."

# Marcus: The First Date

I chose a small, family-owned Italian restaurant ten miles outside the city, the kind of place where the owner still cooked and knew everyone by name. It was far from the glass towers of my world and the high-end steakhouses of hers. I needed neutrality, an authenticity shield. I had booked a table under a generic, unfamiliar last name—not Vance—and paid cash upfront for the small, quiet table in the back.

"It's a long drive for spaghetti, Marcus," she observed, sliding into the booth across from me. She was wearing a simple silk dress, no corporate armor in sight;

her hair was free, hanging down, showing off her fresh retwist that radiated efficiency. She looked like a woman who chose simple elegance over demanding it.

The light in the restaurant was warm, the kind that smelled of oregano and old wood. I ordered a simple red wine and let her choose the pasta—a minor surrender of control that felt strangely freeing.

I kept my movements small, conscious of not making any grand gestures or mentioning any of the exclusive properties I'd just toured today. I asked her about her most significant case, not the victory, but the defeat.

"What did you learn when you lost?" She paused, genuinely thrown by the angle.

"I learned that logic isn't enough. That passion has to be packaged correctly, or it gets dismissed as emotion. And that sometimes, the simple truth is too messy for a jury."

"I know that kind of chaos," I said, choosing my words meticulously. This was the tightrope walk:

speaking the truth of my job without using the title. "Running a fleet—even a small, specialized one—is pure risk management. If one sedan breaks down, I don't just lose a job; I lose a client for life. My nights are spent on logistics, planning routes based on predictive traffic models. I can't afford failure, so I have to be ten steps ahead of the traffic, ten steps ahead of my own team."

Internal Check: Did I say CEO? No. Did I say I owned the fleet? No. Did I describe the work of an ambitious, hands-on operator? Yes.

She leaned forward, her eyes bright with focused interest. "That's high-stakes. It's like arguing a case where the road itself is the opposing counsel. You have to anticipate every single possible move."

"Exactly," I confirmed, savoring the connection. We dissected the concept of control. I spoke about the stress of managing a group of vehicles, the sleepless nights spent handling logistics, and the quiet joy of turning a small, chaotic operation into a functional, thriving entity. Every word I spoke was accurate, detailing the genuine stress and pride of ownership. Still, I omitted the word 'owner' and substituted a group for 'my' in references to the company.

She told me how her colleagues' praise felt hollow; I told her how the silence of my home at night felt colder than any air conditioning unit—another near miss. I corrected 'my penthouse' in my head mid-sentence, catching the slip just in time. I wanted to share the loneliness, but sharing the specific architectural details would ruin the whole premise.

"So you just have it all figured out?" She said with a smile.

"In my head, yes. I have to manifest it outside of my mind. I want to look good next to you at your next work gala."

"You are still trying to get those five stars, I see."

"It's never too late to leave a review."

"I will wait to see how the rest of the night goes. Do you have any kids, Marcus?"

"No, I don't have any kids, but I would like to have some one day."

"Are you not going to ask me if I have any?"

"I don't need to."

"And why is that?"

"You don't have any of the 'I have kids signs." She gave me this look like she wanted me to explain. "In my experience, women who have kids usually have them as the background on their phones or lock screens. They are also constantly checking their phones for texts or missed calls. So it's either I am the most interesting man in the world or you don't have kids. And I am guessing both."

She stared at me with this smile that looked like she was contemplating jumping across the table and kissing me. Her lips were plump, juicy, and the light reflected the shine of the gloss on her lips. Damn, I wanted to taste her lips.

"Four stars," she said. Her eyes were still locked on me.

"That just isn't going to work. What can I do to get that last star?

"You can kiss me." This was it. The moment I have been waiting for. I licked my lips real smooth with my best LL Cool J impression. I leaned in, and her scent sent a longing through my body that made the other senses jealous. If perfection were a person, it wouldn't have shit on her.

I closed the distance and my eyes once I lined up our lips. 'CRASH!' A waiter dropped his whole tray. The moment was stolen, and now it's a little awkward. I left a tip on the table and we left. She noticed I didn't pay, and I told her I had store credit as I opened her door and let her into the car.

By the time I drove her back, the car filled with the soft scent of her perfume, a beautiful lightness had settled over me. We headed back near Uptown to her place. I ran to the other side of the car and opened her door.

"Zahra, I would love to see you again tomorrow, and every day after that."

"Do you have that kind of time?"

"Well, all I do is work. I have some vacation days saved up, and being with you is better than any beach or island."

"Give me your phone," she demanded. She noticed that I didn't have a lock on it. She typed in her real number.

"Call me when you make it home, and we can talk about tomorrow." I gave her the tightest hug I felt she could handle. She fit perfectly in my arms. My hands stopped at the arch of her back, right before her ass started its perfect curve.

I watched her walk up to her door. She stopped, turned around, and said, "Four stars." I did not hesitate this time. Nothing was going to stop me. I walked up to her, and she had her arms down in front, crossed, holding her clutch.

I backed her against the door, my right hand pressed against it, and my left hand went straight under her chin. I gently but firmly pulled her into my kiss as I pinned her against the door. Our lips locked. Hers were so soft. Our tongues were curious. Feeling every part of the other.

I bit her lip and pulled on it a little while my hand moved from her chin down to her neck, with a light squeeze. She let out a soft moan that did it for me. My dick was solid, ready for the warmth. Her hands were still down, so she felt it get hard. She turned her hand over and rubbed the length of it up and down through my pants.

She pulled back and held her hands to my chest. "You need to leave." I could see her fast-paced breathing and the chill bumps on her.

"Ok, Zahra. I will call you when I make it home." She opened the door and went inside.

# Zahra: The First Date

The dinner was a profound relief from the noise of my world. Marcus wasn't flashy. He didn't talk about stocks, sports teams, or his future acquisition goals; he spoke about the mechanics of doing.

His hands, I noticed, were competent—not delicate like the men who only signed contracts, but strong, with the faint, visible lines of someone who occasionally got their hands dirty maintaining the fleet of vehicles.

"Why transportation? It seems so... relentlessly stressful," I'd asked, watching the firelight flicker in his dark eyes. The flickering was mesmerizing, and I found myself studying the subtle changes in his expression as he spoke.

"It's control," he admitted, shrugging, his gaze steady. "Chaos is out there, right? Traffic, weather, bad planning. I like being the thing that moves people through the chaos safely and precisely. It's a very satisfying kind of control. You can't bullshit chaos."

That line—You can't bullshit chaos—struck me harder than any closing argument. It was pure, unvarnished truth. His ambition wasn't abstract; it was grounded in asphalt and engine timing. I listened as he meticulously described the process of anticipating clients' needs, managing vehicle rotations, and dealing with emergency mechanical failures.

He spoke with the authority of someone who had built a system, the diligence of a high-level manager, or perhaps an owner-operator who hadn't forgotten the grind. I respected the sheer effort this implied. It reminded me of my own hustle—the long nights studying law while others were partying. He would be a great asset to any company.

He spoke about missing a free throw in high school, the disappointment was still real. "I didn't lose the game. I lost the opportunity to be perfect. And you can't buy that back."

I felt myself softening. This wasn't a man who had inherited his confidence; he had earned it by fighting for perfection in small, necessary ways. He was out of my league financially, maybe, but he was in a better one entirely—the league of the self-made, the truly ambitious, the true work-hard league, and I wanted every part of it, of him.

"So you just have it all figured out?" I said with a smile.

"In my head, yes. I have to manifest it outside of my mind. I want to look good next to you at your next work gala."

"You are still trying to get those five stars, I see."

"It's never too late to leave a review."

"I will wait to see how the rest of the night goes. Do you have any kids, Marcus?"

"No, I don't have any kids, but I would like to have some one day."

"Are you not going to ask me if I have any?"

"I don't need to."

"And why is that?" I wondered.

"You don't have any of the 'I have kids signs." I gave him this look —like, what bullshit is he about to try to explain to me?

"In my experience, women who have kids usually have them as the background on their phones or lock screens. They are also constantly checking their phones for texts or missed calls. So, it's either I am the most interesting man in the world or you don't have kids. And I am guessing both."

"So how many dates have you been on to gather this much information?"

"Too many," he said with a look of disappointment on his face. "I am hoping that this date will be the start of something lasting for us."

I stared at him, thinking that this man is too good with his words. Everything he said had a hint of confidence and truth, and I was slowly buying into it. The way he wears his confidence is alluring, and I love that he isn't cocky about it.

His beard was moisturized, his skin was glowing, his teeth were perfect, and his waves were on point. To think that I almost let this man get away. I've decided to see this one through.

"Four stars," I said. My eyes were locked on him.

"That just isn't going to work. What can I do to get that last star?

"You can kiss me." I can't believe that I just said that out loud. I was thinking it, but it's out there now. He has a controlled, excited look. He licked his lips real smoothly. It reminded me of how LL Cool J used to do it.

He leaned in, and his scent smelled familiar and new at the same time, like I smelled it before but couldn't put a finger on it. I wanted him to devour me so bad.

He closed the distance, and I closed my eyes once our lips were lined up. 'CRASH!' A waiter dropped his whole tray. The moment was stolen, and now it's a little awkward.

He left a tip on the table, and we left. Wait, I thought to myself, when did he pay for the food? He must have seen the confusion on my face because he told me that he had store credit as he opened my door and helped me into the car.

By the time we made it back to my place, the car filled with the strong scent of his cologne, a fresh cedar-and-spice scent had settled over me. We were near Uptown, where my condo was. He ran to the other side of the car and opened my door.

"Zahra." The way he says my name sends chills up my arms like he knows how to get me there already. "I would love to see you again tomorrow, and every day after that."

"Do you have that kind of time?"

"Well, all I do is work. I have some vacation days saved up, and being with you is better than any beach or island."

"Give me your phone," I demanded. I noticed that he didn't have a lock on his phone. What kind of person does that? I  typed in my real number.

"Call me when you make it home, and we can talk about tomorrow." He gave me the tightest hug. It felt like he was trying to be gentle, but I wanted him to grab my ass and squeeze it. I felt like a perfect fit in his arms. His hands stopped at the arch of my back, right before all this ass starts its perfect curve. We are going to work on this.

I felt him watching as he walked slightly behind me. We made it to my door. I stopped, turned around, and said, "Four stars." I had my hands crossed, trying to look innocent.

He did not hesitate this time. Nothing was going to stop him. He walked up to me so fast that I didn't have time to move my hands.

I felt my back against the door as his hand held our weight to soften the impact. He grabbed my chin and pulled me into a kiss. I was pinned against the door and a hard place. Our lips locked. It felt so good. Our tongues were curious. Feeling every part of the other.

He bit my lip and pulled on it a little while his hand moved from my chin down to my neck, with a light squeeze. I didn't want gentle, not right now. I wanted him to squeeze until my knees gave way. I wanted him to carry me inside and fuck me right on my couch.

I let out a soft moan to let him know he was doing everything right and that it felt good. I felt his dick get hard against the back of my hand that was trapped down there. It was solid, ready for this pussy. I turned my hand around and started to stroke his girth through his pants. I could feel it pulsating in my hands. I could feel his grip tightening around my neck. The visual I just had was about to come true, but I stopped it.

I am not giving this man any of this on the first date. I pulled back and put my hands on his chest. "You need to leave." I could see the length of him going down his thigh. He was just as flustered as I was.

"Ok, Zahra. I will call you when I make it home." I opened the door and went inside.

# Marcus: White Lie

We decided to link uptown for a walk during some downtime a few days later. Everything was going well so far. I was standing at the intersection where we agreed to meet. She came around the corner looking like she jumped straight out of a fitness magazine.

She might as well have nothing on the way her leggings were hugging her thighs and booty. Her smile was infectious. As soon as she did it, I couldn't stop mine from reacting, even though I was trying to play it cool. We gave each other a big hug.

"Let me find out you missed me, hugging me like that," she said jokingly.

"My body needed that. Let me find out that you're walking around the workplace looking like this," I retorted.

"I am done with the office today, so I wanted to be ready for anything you had planned. Is this too much?"

"It's perfect, beautiful."

"Ok, five stars," are the little pet names we decided on, I guess. We started walking, and our hands naturally gravitated towards each other. We felt right for each other. Her early dismissal of me for being a driver was always at the back of my mind. Now wasn't the time to tell her who I really was. I wanted to enjoy her just like this.

I pulled Zahra to a stop beneath a massive oak tree in the sprawling downtown park, the kind of place where city executives shed their blazers and acted like normal people for an hour.

This felt less like a date and more like a soft, high-stakes interrogation, the kind where the only currency was honesty, or at least the calculated performance of it.

"My turn to ask the real questions," she said, sitting on the edge of the fountain, watching the sunlight splinter across the water. "You talk about the job, the hustle, the logistics. But where does that drive come from? Who is Marcus McNair? You don't have the typical background of the men I usually meet."

I smiled, feeling the familiar, tightening knot of the performance begin. This was the moment for the *White Lie*—the truth, trimmed of the risky financial details.

"You're right. No prep schools or trust funds here," I admitted, picking up a smooth, flat stone. This was technically true; I adopted the name Vance later in life.

"When I was ten, my life became a footnote in a tragedy. My mother died in a hit-and-run, and my father... he didn't handle it well. He ended up going away for a long, long time after he killed the driver."

I kept the details vague, letting the pain hang in the air, allowing her to assume the worst. The papers said *McNair*. I didn't clarify that the McNair was the ten-year-old child adopted by a distant family friend, who had the good sense to give me a new name—Vance—and seed money for my first car.

I tossed the stone; it skipped once, then sank. Zahra watched me, her expression soft—not pitying—which was precisely the response I needed. "God, Marcus. That's a lot for a kid to carry."

"It gives you an appreciation for stability," I shrugged. "For making sure the wheels never stop turning."

Then she pivoted, the lawyer in her surfacing. "And where are you staying now? That building you mentioned last time? The one with the bad service."

"It's an apartment near the airport," I confessed, a half-truth that was a half-lie. "It's temporary, until my condo is ready. I'm renovating it right now. I just wanted to make it a little nicer so maybe I could rent it out once I find my forever home."

The condo was my luxury Airbnb unit —one of twelve —but the general concept was true. The temporary apartment was a small, dusty unit I actually kept near the Prime depot for 3 a.m. maintenance checks—a place I used for less than half a year.

I turned the conversation back to her, needing the balance of her truth against my carefully constructed fiction. "Enough about my dark ages. You're the steady one. Tell me about the Hayes family unit."

Her face relaxed, and she spoke with a genuine vulnerability that gutted me.

"They're solid. Predictable. Still together, still annoyingly perfect in the suburbs. My biggest fault, I think, is that I let my world become too rigid. My sister... she's the free spirit. We had a falling out over something stupid years ago. We haven't talked properly since. I miss her. I'm ready to have that conversation, but she's not."

"You're here, aren't you?" I said softly, reaching across the bench to brush a lock of hair from her cheek. "That's the conversation. You're open to the chaos."

She nodded, leaning into my touch. "I am. But I'm terrified of trusting someone who might not be. Letting people in has always been a struggle for me. Even with family."

I held her gaze, feeling the weight of the lie like a physical object in my chest. I had offered her facts stripped of their context, names stripped of their worth. She took it all as genuine vulnerability. For every question, I had a half-truth waiting, and tonight, the deception had worked perfectly. I had passed the test, and the reward was her trust.

# Zahra: Deep Dive

I told myself it was professional diligence. It was standard procedure for anyone entering my orbit. But the truth was, I felt Marcus had given me only a partial truth and a vague account of his life, and the lawyer in me couldn't tolerate the gaps. That night, after a few hours of work on my brief, I found myself on my laptop, typing the name *Marcus McNair* and the city where he said he grew up.

The results were chillingly easy to find, yet horrifying.

He was right: the two worst days of his life were public record. The story, however, was far more brutal than his sparse account implied. His mother's hit-and-run death was confirmed, but the article detailed the police report: the accident wasn't just near him; he was in the back seat of the car when it happened, ten years old, watching the sudden, violent end of his world.

The second news cycle was about his father. Marcus hadn't elaborated on the *long, long time away*. The truth was a life sentence. His father, overwhelmed by grief and rage that the man who killed his wife had managed to make bail, tracked him down and murdered him in a calculated act of vengeance. The father, James McNair, went to prison for life, leaving Marcus, the sole survivor, entirely alone.

My fingers stilled over the keyboard. That wasn't just a tough childhood; it was a trauma of biblical proportions. No wonder the man was obsessed with control, logistics, and stability. He had survived a chaos that most people couldn't comprehend.

Then I found the legal trail. The case had been sealed quickly, but a tiny, archived note on the initial probate filing listed that the only asset recovered was a three-hundred-thousand-dollar life insurance payout from his mother's policy. It was a staggering amount for a ten-year-old in the late 90s, the kind of money that wouldn't make him a tycoon, but indeed placed him miles ahead of the *just-starting* driver he was pretending to be.

The money wasn't a lie; it was a foundational piece of the truth he had deliberately hidden. The money was trauma turned into capital.

Everything else was a dead end. I confirmed Marcus's statement: any social media accounts or anything under 'McNair' led back to the sealed court records, making his excuse about not having a social media presence entirely plausible and genuine.

I stopped digging. Any further search would involve proprietary databases that would flag the query, and I couldn't risk exposing my investigation to him.

I shut the laptop, my hands shaking slightly. I had the facts, the motive, and the proof of his fear. The financial lie wasn't malicious; it was a defensive shield forged in the twin fires of tragedy and betrayal.

I grabbed my phone and called Alicia. "Al. You won't believe what I just found out about Marcus."

"I knew he was on the down low. Ain't no way a man that perfect drops out of nowhere," Alicia blurted out.

"Girl, are you ok? What show were you watching that got you fired up?" I continued with the information.

I laid out the story, the grim details of the accident, the father's vengeance, and the three-hundred-thousand-dollar life insurance payout. I waited for her sharp, lawyerly analysis.

"Okay, so he was a traumatized orphan who inherited a large sum of money, and now he is trying to build an empire with it," Alicia summarized calmly. "He's not a con man, Zahra. He's a deeply wounded man who thinks money is a magnet for the exact kind of heartbreak he's already experienced."

"But I know he has the money, Al. Should I ask him about the payout? About the condo? I looked up the location, and there is no way he can afford that on his salary," I pressed, the legal urge to demand disclosure overwhelming me.

Alicia sighed, the sound crackling over the phone line. "You're trying to put him on the stand. Stop being the lawyer for five minutes, Zahra. He just gave you his soul on a cracked park bench. You now know his deepest, most painful truth.

He's afraid of being judged for the money because every woman before you *only* judged him on the money. Let's not forget that you did just that. Stop putting him on trial for the one thing he's trying to get away from. Be in the moment. Be the safe space."

She was right. I was using my intelligence as a weapon, not as a source of compassion. I had to let the discovery be my burden, not his.

# Marcus: The Locker Room Confessional

The next evening, the three of us were back on the cracked asphalt court, playing a tense, fast-paced game of twenty-one. I was dominating, running on the sheer adrenaline left over from the date. Gary was sweating profusely; Lee was loudly complaining that my in-and-out move was a carry.

"You're playing like you got it in last night, Marcus! What did you do, offer her a lifetime subscription to Prime?" Lee yelled, wiping sweat from his forehead.

"Better," I gasped, stealing the ball from Gary and sinking a long fadeaway. "I told her everything about my past. Well, just enough for her to do some digging. Our schedules are both tight, but we talk on the phone every day, and we are taking a trip next month to celebrate us."

Gary caught his breath. "So, the facade held up. What did you talk about? You didn't slip up and mention any of your properties, did you?"

"Are you kidding? I was on maximum verbal lockdown except for the condo," I panted, leaning on the ball. "We talked about life and ambitions. I kept using phrases like 'when the fleet is running right' and 'the margins are tight on every run.' Every time she asked a big-picture question, I framed it in terms of execution and hustle, not ownership and exit strategy."

Lee whistled. "That's genius. You basically described your day without using the word 'boss nigga.' What about where you live? She must have asked."

"I told her I lived in a building with a great view and bad service. Which is true," I said, shrugging. The service in my own penthouse complex was notoriously slow. "She saw the work in me, Gary. The real, grinding ambition that built Prime from the ground up, not the sanitized executive version. She saw the cost of the success, not the reward."

Gary took the ball from me, his expression turning serious. "That's what you wanted, man. But you're building your dream home on a fault line. You established honesty by being dishonest about the one thing that will change everything. Are you prepared for the inevitable crash out when she finds out the cost is actually a multimillion-dollar company?"

I looked at the ground, tracing the chalk line with my shoe. "I'll cross that bridge when I have to. For now, I have a beach vacation with a woman who likes me because I'm passionate about preventing people from getting stuck in traffic. And that is enough for me right now," I grinned, tossing the ball to Lee. "Hit the showers, gentlemen. I need to spend the next two weeks crafting the perfect itinerary for a scenic drive down the coast in a month."

Gary walked up and grabbed my shoulders. "What does she get out of this? A rich liar. What makes you better than the men she has already dated like you? The ones that feel like the rules of life don't apply to them. Like one stroke of a pen will make it all go away. This is not you."

I looked at him. "You are right, my dude. I will tell her when we go to the beach." I need to figure out how.

# Zahra: The Unqualified Opinion

The spin class was brutal, the music deafening, but the effort felt cleansing. Alicia and I were cooling down on the mats afterward, both drenched in sweat.

"I'm telling you, Al, I've never been this relaxed after a first date or doing a deep dive," I said, stretching my hamstring. The usual post-date analysis of Did he mean that? Is he going to call? Was completely absent. These last few months have been great.

"Relaxed because you're not dating a partner who can quote the firm's third quarter earnings better than you can, or relaxed because he doesn't represent a threat to your autonomy, or relaxed because he stretched you out last night?" Alicia countered, ever the insightful one.

"You got two out of the three!"

"Please say one of them is that he stretched you out."

"No! He's just... grounded. He's obsessed with precision and execution—the language I speak—but he applies it to the tangible world of moving cars and managing mechanical risk, not abstract equity law. He actually talked about the physical effort of keeping his future small fleet running and what he wanted out of life and who he would like to have it with, and everything felt genuine."

I closed my eyes, recalling the warmth of the small restaurant, the smell of oregano, and how hard he was in my hand. "He has the focus of a CEO, but the humility of a driver. He wasn't trying to sell me anything. He asked me about my failures, Al. Not my victories. Who does that?" Alicia looked skeptical but intrigued.

"Okay, so he's ambitious, but the corporate hamster wheel does not drive him. That's good. But we have to talk about the reality of the income gap, Zahra. You pull down high-six figures, maybe more with bonuses. He's driving. You're dating him because he's authentic, but are you prepared for the logistics of the lifestyle disparity? Have you found out what he did with the three-hundred-thousand-dollar life insurance payout?"

I sighed, the question hitting a familiar, painful nerve. "I know. I thought about that. I asked myself whether I could handle being the primary earner —the one who buys the tickets, the one who pays for the nicer vacation. And honestly? I think I can. It's worth it for the integrity. I don't want a partner who needs my money, but I'd rather date someone with an honest paycheck and integrity than someone with a trust fund and a private jet. The insurance is only important for how he handles money."

"But will he be able to handle it?" Alicia pointed out, tapping my arm. "He sounds deeply proud of his hard work. If he's constantly faced with the fact that your success easily dwarfs his, that pride could turn into resentment. You have to be careful not to make him feel small, even accidentally. It's a delicate ego management operation, counselor."

I chewed on that for a minute. That was the qualified opinion, the legal risk assessment. It was valid. But the memory of his genuine laugh and the intelligent darkness in his eyes was a powerful counterargument.

"I can manage a delicate ego, Al. It's certainly easier than managing a liar. Besides, he drives a clean, high-end SUV. He's not struggling. He's just... starting out. And I genuinely believe he's going to be successful one day. I'm betting on the hustle, on him."

# Marcus: The Trip

The first short trip we took was a weekend drive down the coast. I chose a comfortable, unmarked SUV from the fleet, its suspension designed to devour miles without jarring the passenger. I drove her to a hidden bluff overlooking the Atlantic, a place I'd discovered years ago while scouting for expansion options. We were a little over 4 months in at this point

She sat next to me in the passenger seat. Her beauty had no limits. The sunlight caught the fabric, making the blue-and-white tropical floral print shimmer as the sun came through the window. She wore a simple halter-neck triangle bikini paired with a matching, sheer sarong, tied loosely at her hip. The breezy wrap offered just enough coverage for a stroll to the water's edge, creating a vibrant, effortlessly chic look perfect for a hot summer day.

The car's silence was beautiful, filled with the comforting sound of the ocean wind whipping past the windows.

"You know these backroads like you come here often," she teased, watching me downshift expertly on a steep, winding curve.

"I know the quickest route to any place you want to be," I said, letting the words hang with a dual meaning that made her smile widen.

It was during that drive that we got intimate. Not physically, but intellectually. The low, golden light of the afternoon sun slanted across the leather interior, and she finally, truly opened up.

She told me about the ethical compromises she had to make daily—the moral fatigue of defending corporate greed—and the quiet, painful longing to argue a case that mattered to people, not profits.

"I feel like I'm constantly arguing the wrong side," she confessed, staring out at the hazy blue of the ocean. "I'm great at it. But I feel empty."

I pulled the car over onto the gravel shoulder of the bluff and killed the engine. The only sound was the crash of the waves far below.

"You're not fighting the wrong side. You're fighting for control. You want the logic and the rules to matter. You want to make sense of the chaos, just like I do. The difference is, you're trying to find the one moral exception, and I'm just trying to keep the wheels turning on time."

We got out of the SUV and leaned against the hood as we watched the sunset. "Do you always know the right things to say?"

"I try my best to be intentional with everything I do and say when it comes to you."

I held her gaze, letting the intensity build in the small, confined bubble called us in this big world. "You can't fix the world, Zahra. But you can be honest about the fight you're in."

It was the most honest advice I'd ever given her, and the irony—that I was lying while urging her toward truth—twisted in my gut. But the look in her eyes, the gratitude and the sudden closeness, made the lie feel necessary, like a protective membrane around something fragile and new.

We stood there against the SUV watching the sun go down. My back was against the vehicle. Her back was on my chest, and her ass was perfectly placed on something that was waking up. She leaned her head back to rest on my shoulders. I had my arms wrapped around her, and her hands were on mine.

She felt me getting hard and started to slowly move her booty from left to right like we were slow dancing. She looked up at me, and we kissed. Everything right here, right now, was perfect. Oh shit, how can I tell her the truth?

The sun was starting to drop toward the horizon as we continued toward the inn. We decided to stop at a small, open-air beach bar for a couple of quick drinks. The place was lively, filled with tourists and local business types celebrating the end of the week.

We sat at a table facing the water, the music a pleasant, low thrum. I watched her as she ordered, her face relaxed, her hand naturally resting near mine on the weathered wood table.

I felt a surge of genuine joy, the kind that had nothing to do with market cap or acquisition targets. I was just happy on a date. Then her expression froze. Her eyes flicked past my shoulder toward the entrance, and the transformation was immediate and jarring.

"Oh, God. It's Dennis and Tara," she murmured, her voice flattening instantly into the calm, professional tone I hated. She pulled her hand back, placing it precisely on her lap. "They're from the firm's real estate litigation team. Big partners. Just... be cool."

"Just be cool?" I repeated.

"Yes, just let me do the talking."

I didn't need to look. I could feel the shift in the air pressure around us, the sudden emergence of the high-stakes world she usually left behind. Dennis, a man in a matching short set, and Tara, sharp as a tack, approached our table.

"Zahra! Fancy seeing you out here. We're celebrating the Sterling settlement," Dennis boomed, barely glancing at me.

Zahra rose, the picture of professional composure. "Dennis, Tara. That's excellent news. This is Marcus. He... drove me down for the weekend."

"Maybe he can give us a ride back to our room," Dennis said jokingly. Already lit.

"Or maybe he can just give me a ride or let me." Dennis and Tara busted out laughing. They both were clearly buzzed. These are the people she was ashamed to have me meet. To know what we are.

She didn't offer a handshake, didn't mention my name again, and delivered the introduction with the casual finality of a court dismissal.

I forced a polite, easy smile. "Pleasure. I handle logistics down the coast. Are you enjoying the win?"

Tara, ever the predator, fixed her gaze on me, taking in my simple, good-quality but understated polo shirt. "Logistics? Excellent. Good drivers are hard to find." She turned her attention immediately back to Zahra.

"We were just discussing the acquisition terms for the new office tower. You really should swing by and say hello later."

For the next ten minutes, they spoke over and around me as if I were a particularly well-dressed piece of furniture. Zahra maintained a physical and verbal cordon around herself, keeping me firmly on the perimeter of her attention.

Every question I asked her was answered with a brief, efficient sentence, and then she pivoted back to a discussion of commercial leases. The genuine warmth that had defined our last couple of months vanished, replaced by the dazzling, cold precision of the corporate lawyer.

I felt a bitter sting, a deep humiliation that reached beyond the performance. It wasn't just that she wouldn't touch me; it was that she wouldn't even look at me with the same affection she'd shown moments before. The driver persona was a costume, and she was terrified of her peers seeing her dancing with the help.

I finally excused myself to the bar, muttering something about a phone call. She just said ok and went back to her conversation.

"Make sure she gets home safe," Tara said as I walked off. When the partners left, Zahra came over, her expression tight with forced relief.

"Thank you. That was painful. They're vultures," she hissed, grabbing my hand, then quickly letting go.

"It was humiliating," I said, my voice low and controlled, resisting the urge to be witty. "You just put on a show that redefined the word distant. What, were you afraid Dennis would think you were dating someone who had to work for a living or was just a driver?"

The words hit her, the color draining from her face. I grabbed my keys out of her purse. "We're leaving. Now."

The drive to the inn was silent for five miserable miles, the tension in the car thick and toxic. I was furious, and I drove faster than necessary, the powerful engine a low, frustrated growl.

"Slow down, please! Marcus. You're driving like a maniac," she finally snapped, clutching the console. "Can we talk about it?"

I slammed on the brakes, pulling the car onto the shoulder of the dark, coastal highway. The sudden silence was absolute. I turned to face her, the soft light from the dashboard illuminating her profile.

"I've never felt so dismissed in my life, Zahra. I'm just the driver who drove you down? So, tell me, why did you spend thirty minutes treating me like I was invisible back there? Because they're vultures? Or because you were terrified of them seeing you with someone who doesn't fit into your carefully manicured world?"

She looked away, folding her arms tight across her chest. "Don't you dare question me about that. You don't know what you're talking about. Why are you making such a big deal about this?"

"Because it is! I know exactly what I'm talking about! You want the easy honesty I give you, but you can't handle the inconvenient truth of where I stand in the food chain! You preach authenticity, but you just spent thirty minutes lying to your own face! Why even go through this if you are afraid to love me in public?"

She finally met my eyes, and the sheer desperation in her gaze made my anger falter.

"You're right! You're completely right!" she admitted, the words spilling out, laced with a raw fear that sounded nothing like the lawyer. "I was scared, am scared. I was terrified. Not because of where you are in the food chain, but because I'm falling for you, Marcus, and you're the first person I've trusted enough to let close since college!"

She leaned forward, her hands clenched. "No one tells the full truth in my world, Marcus. Everyone is hiding the ugly parts, the compromise, the cost. You're hiding something big—I know you are, I can feel it. And I don't know what the full truth is. Still, I know that if I let myself be affectionate with the 'driver' in front of my world, and then you turn out to be another liar, another massive, sophisticated disappointment, I don't know how I'll recover. I'm scared of being hurt, because I'm letting go of control, and you're proving I shouldn't! Maybe I am self-sabotaging, maybe I am going through that this is too good to be true stage. I have been on the defensive my entire life, and it's hard for me to turn it off, but with you, I want to rest my case and be loved, but I am scared, Marcus."

Tears came down her cheek. The sheer admission of vulnerability took my breath away. She wasn't angry; she was terrified of the impending betrayal she sensed. My entire, elaborate plan had just run headlong into her deepest, most guarded fear.

"I won't hurt you," I whispered, reaching for her hand and wiping her tears. Her hand was cold, shaking slightly. "I promise you, I will never intentionally hurt you. I am all in with you, Z, but I need you to be all in with me as well. I don't want to be the driver when we meet friends, family, and coworkers. I want to be your man, your lover, your everything."

She looked at me, a lawyer assessing the credibility of a witness under oath. "I am so sorry if I made you feel belittled or invisible. I promise I will never do that again. You are my man, Marcus. I need to know, what are you not telling me?"

# Zahra: The Vulnerability

The seaside trip felt like a profound reset button for my life. For the first time, I was purely relaxed, trusting Marcus's competence implicitly. Sitting in the passenger seat, letting him navigate, was the ultimate surrender of control—a powerful, almost frightening sign of faith for a high-stakes litigator.

But the encounter at the beach bar had ripped that illusion to shreds. My automatic withdrawal, the instantaneous erection of the corporate wall between Marcus and my peers, was a self-betrayal more acute than any lie I thought that he was telling. And the argument on the highway—his fury, my terrifying admission—left me shaken to the core.

"I'm scared of being hurt, because I'm letting go of control, and you're proving I shouldn't!"

That raw, honest scream of fear was the truth I had spent fifteen years burying beneath billable hours and flawless courtroom composure. Why does this man have so much control over my mind and my heart?

I feel like he is an unforgivable risk, but my fear was the true weakness. He wasn't the risk; the risk was my own willingness to believe him and let him in. What if he is right for me, and I am forcing an issue when there is none?

When we finally made it to the simple, rustic inn, the air between us was heavy with the unresolved argument, thick with fear and promise.

I asked him about his future, probing gently. "What's the endgame, Marcus? Do you want to own the biggest fleet in the state? The country?"

He took a slow sip of wine, the sound crisp. "I don't need the biggest. I need the best run, the most reliable fleet. My endgame is stability. A business that runs itself perfectly so that I can spend my time on things and people that actually matter."

I leaned in, my voice low, my entire focus fixed on his answer. "Like what or who?" He sat on the couch beside me.

His hand reached for mine, his touch warm and deliberate, his thumb tracing the sharp line of my knuckles. "Like proving to a cynical, smart corporate lawyer that not every ambitious person is a liar." He leaned in and kissed my cheek slowly.

The conviction in his voice made me believe him completely. I finished my wine, the glass feeling suddenly too heavy. The truth was that my defensive control was tiring. And Marcus, the driver, was permitting me to set it down.

"Show me," I whispered, not as a challenge, but as a demand. My last moment of control that I relinquished to him.

He didn't speak. He stood, his movement slow and sure, and offered me his hand. The touch was steady, the callouses from years of driving and maintenance providing a texture far more real than the smooth, soft palms of the executives I usually dated.

We moved into the small, quiet room, the only light coming from the crack of the porch door, painting the air a hazy, deep blue. I didn't need the grand chandelier or the city view; I only needed the clean sheets and the sound of the ocean, a massive, honest roar that swallowed the little lies of the city.

I turned to him, and he took my face in his hands, his thumbs grazing my cheekbones. There was no cleverness in his eyes now, only a terrifying, focused intensity that looked right into the messy, vulnerable parts of my soul.

"No performance," he murmured, his voice husky. "Just me. Just us. I'm giving you the truth you demanded, Zahra. Now, stop being afraid of it."

I pulled his shirt to me, needing the confirmation of his physical presence. His kiss was a slow, careful acknowledgment, the opposite of the aggressive, entitled hunger I was used to. It was a negotiation without words, a mutual surrender, and I was losing the battle as his tongue swirled in my mouth.

His hands moved with an easy competence, unwrapping the armor I wore all day—first the sleek silk gown I put on after the shower, then the subtle tension around my neck and shoulders that never left me in the courtroom.

For the first time, I felt utterly seen, stripped bare of my title and my carefully constructed competence. He admired the strength in my body, the ambition in my spirit, but he demanded my complete, honest relaxation.

As my gown hit the floor, he moved his lips from mine and onto my neck. His left hand pulled my hair back gently to fully expose my neck, and his other hand was on my ass. He squeezed it nice and hard. The pain felt so damn good.

He licked and bit on my neck like he was starving for me. The way he sucked on my neck, I felt like I would turn into a vampire any minute and be team Marcus forever. All I could do was moan, "Yes, baby."

It was sensory overload. I felt his tongue on my neck, his hand on the bottom of my ass, squeezing as he took his finger and rubbed it back and forth over the lips of my pussy. My breast was pressed against his hard chest.

I reached down to stroke his dick, but he stopped me. "I'm in control, you told me to show you." In one swift motion, I was off my feet. He put both hands between my legs and lifted me by my ass. My breast was right in his face. I put my hands on his shoulders as he took turns on each breast, sucking and licking each nipple.

I closed my eyes; it felt like I was flying through a cloud of pleasure. He was able to slide one of his long, fat fingers inside me. I could feel it pressing against my spot. He moved his finger in and out and back and forth.

I leaned my head back and drove my nails into his back as I could feel myself getting wet on this man's finger. I could hear the sound it made as he moved his finger back and forth. He didn't give me time to recover.

He spun me around and laid me down gently on the bed. He crawled on the bed like a sniper getting in position for the perfect headshot, and my clit was the target.

He held both of my legs open with his hands and started licking my clit. He was going so fast. He would switch it up from fast light flicks to heavy, slow circles. I couldn't decide which one I liked better. I just moaned. I grabbed his head and pulled him in closer. He opened his mouth and stuck his tongue out flat and wide.

I started to rock my hips back and forth. He looked up at me and said, "You like it, baby?"

"Yes, baby, I love it." He started sucking and doing circles with his tongue as an orgasm began to build. He must have felt it too because he gripped me tighter and kept this constant pace that was more than enough to get me there.

I let out another loud moan as I exploded with pleasure. Sensitivity immediately came over me. He kept going as wave after wave of the orgasm pulsated through my body. When I looked up, he was already naked and wiping my wetness off his beard. He was long and hard, and my body was craving for it.

He grabbed me by both of my legs and pulled me to the edge of the bed. I felt weightless compared to his strength. It felt good not to be in control. He slid me to the edge of the bed. My ass was hanging off of it, and he held my legs up by the ankles with one hand.

I watched as he guided the head towards me. He did such an amazing job getting me wet, I knew there would be little resistance to him. My body tightened as I anticipated it penetrating me. The head entered, slowly stretching and filling me up. My hands immediately clutched the sheets.

The slight curve of it was perfect. I could feel it rubbing against my walls and jumped as it went over my spot. He pulled out and started to work it in and out. When I thought it was all in, I could feel it go deeper. I put my hands out to slow his progress because this depth to my body was new to me. He allowed me this much control.

He kept the same pace until I moved my hands. He took my legs and put them on each of his shoulders as his stroke increased. He knew what he was doing. He folded my legs back. I was thanking Alicia for making me do yoga with her. He leaned in for a kiss as he started stroking faster and harder. All the years I spent in school, and the only words that I could say at this moment were, "Yes… Oh… That feels so good, baby."

He raised back up and held my legs out with his hands again. He started to do deep, hard thrusts. I looked down and watched the whole length of him go inside me. Covered in my wetness.

"Hold your legs," he demanded. I reached down, grabbed my legs behind the knee, and pulled them back.

He put two fingers in his mouth and started playing with my clit as he was inside me.

"Oh my God, yes!" I let out as I moaned yes repeatedly. I kept dropping my legs. Being fucked like this and holding them was too much for me to stay on the task he had given me. I let go of my legs and started to grab the sheets again.

That must have lit a fire in him. He turned me over to where my entire body was on the bed, and he was behind me in a few seconds. He pushed the top of my back down to where my face was in the pillows, and my hands were still trying to figure out what just happened. I could feel his hands lift my hips, and he slid it back inside me. My back arched as he traced my spine with his hand.

He was stroking so hard and fast. I could feel his balls slapping against my clit, which just added to the pleasure. He grabbed my hips on both sides and kept pounding. I looked back and saw him watching my ass bounce off his dick. "Yes, baby! Yes." I moaned and exhaled as I released another orgasm. It wasn't as powerful as the first one, but it still felt mind-blowing.

"Oh shit shit shit shit!" He pulled out, but my body was still stuck in the motion. He came all on my ass and back. I felt the warmth of it as we both collapsed on the bed. He took a couple of breaths and went to the bathroom. I assumed he was disposing of his condom.

I heard the water running as my body was still coming down off its orgasmic high. "I got this for you," he said as he entered the room and put a scorching hot towel on my back to clean his cum up.

"What the hell are you doing!" I jumped up.

"Is it too hot? I am sorry, babe." All I could do was laugh at him. He joined in as we both laughed about the hot towel. I snatched it from him and went into the bathroom to turn on the shower. He slapped my ass when I walked by him. Is it weird that I have been waiting for the right person to smack my ass like that?

My eyes were closed as the shower water hit my face like a downpour. The scent of the cucumber melon bodywash was overtaking the room. The shower door opened, and Marcus stepped in. My eyes observed his muscles and physique. All of his tattoos were hidden under his professional appearance at all times, except for when I see him like this —just us.

"Let me get your back," he said. I walked to him and started kissing his chest, tracing his tattoos. He was a work of art. I reached down and grabbed him. My hand barely made it around his girth. I started to moan, stroke it, and kiss him as I felt it get hard in my hand. Once it was ready, I turned around, bent over for him, and said, "Yes, you can take care of my back."

# Marcus: Game Night

The game night was supposed to be the victory lap. Zahra and I were approaching six months in, established, intimate. The lie had calcified into a comfortable routine. She was laughing with Gary over a ridiculous card game, Lee was attempting to teach Alicia how to shuffle like a Las Vegas dealer, and I was leaning against the marble counter, watching Zahra.

She was radiant, her corporate armor entirely shed, talking about law and life with a genuine ease I rarely saw in her own office. This was what I fought for. This feeling of normal.

My friends had adapted beautifully. Gary stuck to logistics talk, keeping Lee in check. I was still Marcus, the ambitious transport guy, making enough money to afford this upscale apartment and these friends, but nothing that screamed "tycoon." It was perfect.

Tonight would be the night that I take off my mask and tell her who I really am. I hope what we have built so far will be strong enough to withstand the hurricane of emotions about to hit it.

"We got your back, Marcus," Gary said as he and Lee walked over.

"Yeah, my brother, whatever happens, we won't laugh in your face for being an idiot and not telling her sooner," Lee added.

"You are right, fellas. Whatever happens tonight is on me," I said with a hint of regret.

"Alicia, baby, when is your friend getting here?" Lee yelled across the room. "I'm starting to feel like a fifth wheel, the way you and Gary keep eye fucking each other."

"Boy bye! Ain't you nobody worrying about you or Gary. She will get here when she gets here."

"And she better not be ugly." I looked down in embarrassment over Lee's inability to hold his tongue.

"If she were ugly, you would still try to hit. Stop running from this ass whooping in spades and sit back down." Everyone started laughing. We came back to the table with drinks in hand. I kissed Zahra and sat down next to her.

"After this hand, let's hit the balcony so we can talk in private."

"Okay, baby. Is everything ok?"

"Yes, everything is good, bae." I was hoping that would be enough for now, until the doorbell rang.

I felt a cold knot form in my stomach. "Ninety minutes late. Classic," I muttered, but the internal alarm bells were screaming. I knew that sound, that specific, calculated tardiness.

Alicia went to the door. "That'll be Mia, I told her she had to come. You guys need more women in your orbit."

Gary and Lee both looked at me. I felt my stomach drop deeper into my body. There is no way that this is...

I had no time to move, no time to execute a contingency plan. The front door opened, and Mia walked in, pausing in the elegant foyer. She was dressed like a challenge: sharp, expensive, and utterly unimpressed.

Her eyes swept the room—the comfortable luxury, the warmth, the ease—and then they landed on me. For a split second, I saw confusion, a flicker of *Why are you here?*

Then, her features sharpened, twisting into a knowing, calculated smirk that chilled me far more than any boardroom confrontation. She recognized what was going on immediately.

She accepted a glass of wine from Alicia, her gaze never leaving mine. I could feel the sweat prickling my neck. I tried to flash a warning look at Gary, but he was already too focused on the card game. The air suddenly felt too thick to breathe. I was trapped.

"Hey girl, I am glad you made it," Alicia said.

"Thanks for the invite. I was going to go to bed and rub my feet together, but when you told me about tonight, I just had to see it for myself."

Mia walked into the room and began looking around. "This is a nice place you have here, Marcus. What is this, like your fifth or sixth one?"

Mia took a slow, deliberate sip of her wine. She set the glass down with a precise, chilling click. Her eyes fixed on Zahra, who was smiling, entirely unaware.

"Oh, so you two know each other," Alicia said. "Did he drive you around before?"

"Yes, that and other things." She paused for maximum effect, her voice rising just loud enough to cut through the casual chatter.

"Mia, so nice to see you again. It's been a very, very long time, right?" Lee tried to run interference. I could feel Zahra's eyes burning a hole in my face.

"Now would be a great time to say something," Zahra said to me.

"Mia, you need to leave now. You are not supposed to be anywhere near me."

"What are you going to do this time, Marcus? Hit me again, and use your company funds for another settlement. Where am I supposed to go if you keep buying up the city?"

"That's not what happened, and you know it. I settled because I didn't want the bad press, not because it was true. You haven't changed one bit."

"That's where you are wrong, Marcus, that settlement made me a millionaire."

"Marcus, what the fuck is she talking about, and how can you afford something like that if you are just a driver?" Zahra yelled at me.

"Mia, you need to leave now. Zahra, baby, I promise I will explain everything," I tried to console her, but she backed away from me.

"Just the driver, you know, he owns the whole company right? Prime Executive Transport. He's been a millionaire since before I walked out on him five years ago, calling him 'unstable.' Marcus Vance is a master manipulator. He likes  to dress up as the good guy, but he is far from it."

# Zahra: Fight or Flight

The sound of my own laugh was still echoing when Mia delivered the line. It wasn't slurred or drunk; it was clear, sharp, and utterly devastating. The words *millionaire* and *manipulator* were secondary to the sheer, stunning force of the *lie*.

My entire body went cold. The laughter died in my throat, replaced by a searing, white-hot silence. I didn't look at Mia; I looked straight at Marcus.

He was still leaning against the counter, his face a mask of complete, genuine panic. His quick, clever mind, the one I had fallen in love with, had finally failed him. He was cornered, exposed, and suddenly, he looked small.

"Marcus," I managed, the word a razor against my tongue. The room felt like it was spinning, the marble floor suddenly unstable. The details of our dates, the sex, the talk of his *fleet of twenty cars,* the sleepless nights managing *logistics*, suddenly snapped into brutal clarity. Every word he had spoken was accurate, yet entirely false. He had driven a lie, not a car.

"What the hell is she talking about? You didn't trust me enough to tell me the truth?" My voice was low, vibrating with an intensity that drew everyone's attention in the room. The question wasn't about the money, but about the assumption that I was the kind of woman who needed to be tricked.

"Z, let me explain. I'm sorry, I wanted to make sure this was real before I told you who I really was."

"Before we had sex wasn't a good time! When you made me feel bad at the beach bar wasn't a good time! Or how about when I told you that this was the same shit that I was afraid of!"

"Zahra, please, you have to understand where I am coming from. I had to make sure that I wasn't being used."

"Are you this selfish? I fucking feel used and lied to right now, but as long as you are good and not being used, that's all that matters. I don't have time for this. I'm leaving."

"Zahra, wait, let's talk about this." He reached for my arm as I pulled it away from his reach.

"Don't fucking touch me." Alicia and his friends walked between us.

I didn't wait for his inevitable, clever explanation. I couldn't. The physical presence of the lie was overwhelming. I snatched my coat, my vision blurred not by tears, but by pure, incandescent betrayal. I grabbed my purse, the crushing feeling of the shattered game pieces on the counter reflecting the fragments of our relationship.

I walked out the door, leaving the wreckage behind. I could hear Alicia calling my name, but I didn't stop. The clean, cold night air was a shock against the betrayal burning in my chest. The humiliation was secondary to the profound disappointment.

I had finally let my guard down for a man who seemed to value my mind and spirit over my net worth, only to discover that the man was the performance. It wasn't about the money; it was about the deliberate deceit. He had driven a wedge of distrust into the one pure thing I'd found.

# Marcus: Regret

Two days later, the air over Lake Travis was unnaturally still. The silence should have been comforting, but it felt oppressive. I wasn't fishing. I was skipping stones with a frantic, wasted energy that belonged on a basketball court.

Lee pulled his line from the water, sighing dramatically. "So, the empire crumbles not with a market correction, but with a rogue ex-girlfriend and a Pinot-fueled truth bomb. Classic."

I launched a stone that skipped seven times before plunging. "It's not funny, Lee."

"He's just trying to lighten the mood, Marcus," Gary said, his voice calm and level. He set his rod down. "But he's not wrong. You were having too much fun with the facade. You engineered her to like the simple version of you, but the simple version wasn't the whole truth. And a relationship built on a deliberate omission is still built on a lie."

I stopped throwing stones. "She said I was out of her league, Gary. Me. I just... I wanted to see how long I could go before the money complicated things. It was the most normal thing that has happened to me in ten years."

"So that is what this is about? She hurt your entitled feelings, and you just had to prove you could bag her without the money. Look where that has gotten you."

Lee chimed in, leaning forward with a conspiratorial wink. "So, easy fix. You need a big, big gesture. Maybe you buy her a small, underdeveloped island and rename it 'The Island of Trust.' Or you send a fleet of cars. The 'Apology Armada.' Write 'I'm Sorry' on the side in gold leaf."

I shook my head, the suggestion ringing hollow. "No. I did the spectacle. I am the spectacle. And that's why she left. She's a lawyer; she respects proof and consistency. She doesn't want a dazzling closing argument. She wants the evidence. She wants the small, daily effort that proves I'm not running a game."

Gary nodded slowly, confirming my emerging self-awareness. "That's right. You wanted her to value the man, but you showed up wearing the driver's uniform. You need to strip away the uniform and stop trying to be clever. The only challenge here is to be honest and your authentic self, and that shouldn't be the hardest thing you've ever had to do."

I looked out at the water, finally seeing the reflection of my own frustration. "I'm not sending a fleet, Lee. I'm sending a text. And then another, and another. I have to find a way back, one honest word at a time."

***

I was going crazy on the ride home. Every time my phone rang or buzzed, my heart skipped a beat. I was waiting for a text or a call from her. She didn't block me yet, so that was a plus.

My way wasn't working. Surely two days is enough time for someone to get over something that wasn't terrible, right? Maybe I should do something out of the norm. Maybe Lee was onto something.

I drove to the nearest florist to find some of the flowers I remembered her talking about. I walked into the store and saw two women behind the counter.

"Good evening, ladies. When is your next shipment coming in?"

One of the women responded, "We have a truck coming in tomorrow. Can we help you find something?"

"Yes, I want everything."

"Everything?" The other woman repeated.

"I would like to buy every flower arrangement in here, plus some curated with specific flowers and a card," I added as I pulled my black card.

"She must be a very special woman, or you have a lot of making up to do." One of the women said as she started working on my order.

"It's both."

# Zahra: Ambushed

The scent of the flowers—tuberose and gardenia, precisely what I'd mentioned loving during a long, late drive near the coast—hit me first. Then the sheer audacity of the illegally parked car, the trunk open like a shrine. My team stopped dead, murmuring about the disruption. I ignored them, my eyes fixed on the handwritten note.

*I don't need the car or money. I need my passenger princess back. I'm sorry I wasn't honest with you, Zahra. Let me earn your trust back.*

The cleverness was still there, but muted, submerged beneath a desperate sincerity. Before I could process the irony of the gesture—a grand display of wealth and access used to apologize for hiding wealth and access—Marcus appeared from behind a statue at the courthouse.

He was in a perfectly tailored charcoal suit, the kind I knew cost more than my entire month's mortgage, and yet, standing there without the driver's cap, he looked smaller, defenseless.

"Zahra." His voice was rough, quiet enough that the courthouse bustle easily swallowed it.

I carefully folded the note, my movements precise, professional. "You risked a fine and a tow, all for a floral display. That is peak Marcus."

"I risked everything that matters to me for a chance to look you in the eye, plus Sheriff Banks owed me a favor," he countered, his hands hanging stiffly at my sides. "There's no clever angle here. Just me."

I finally looked at him, my gaze a precise weapon. "You wanted me to fall for the real you, right? The honest guy? The ambitious one who takes pride in a hard day's work?"

"Yes. And I was selfish enough to believe that lying to you was the only way to get you there."

"The lie, Marcus, wasn't the money. The lie was the man. You built our relationship on deception and called it intimacy. I am a corporate lawyer. I fight against misrepresentation every day. Do you understand how this looks to me? I shouldn't have to deal with this shit in my personal life as well." My voice didn't rise, which made it far more devastating.

"I do. It looks like I was a coward who couldn't handle the inevitable judgment. Mia used me, and I was used by every other woman who saw dollar signs first. And I was so terrified of losing the one woman who didn't seem to care about the money, I ruined the very thing I was trying to keep."

I took a deep, shaky breath, my eyes softening only slightly. "The flowers are beautiful, Marcus. The note is the only truthful thing you've ever said to me. But a single grand gesture doesn't rebuild trust. It's an easy, spectacular apology that requires no sustained effort. Trust is built day by day, on small things. On showing up when you don't need to. On being quiet when you could be clever."

I straightened my suit jacket. My team was watching, but I didn't care. "I have a case that starts shortly. I can't be distracted by a broken heart right now. I have to win."

I started to walk past him, then stopped, glancing back at the flowers.

"If you want to earn my trust, Marcus, give me some space. Don't send flowers. Don't send texts. Don't show up for coffee. And for God's sake, find a way to be the driver and a millionaire at the same time."

# Zahra: The Verdict

The heavy bronze doors of the courtroom seemed to shut with a finality that had nothing to do with the bailiff and everything to do with my internal state. I walked to the counsel table, my briefcase clicking against the wood with sharp, businesslike precision. I didn't look at my team. I didn't look at the opposition, who were already smugly reviewing their notes. I looked only at the clean, blank page of my legal pad. I have to win.

I pushed Marcus out, stacking the files of my brief like a physical barrier between myself and the ache in my chest. Yet, every argument I prepared, every counterpoint

I mentally rehearsed, was filtered through the lens of betrayal.

*The opposing counsel's entire argument is built on a deliberately misleading financial statement.* It wasn't about the money. It was about the misrepresentation. *Just like him.* I fought the urge to press the folded note in my pocket.

When the judge called the courtroom to order, my mind snapped into the familiar, glorious focus of combat. I was built for this. For the next two hours, the only deception that mattered was the one in front of the court. My voice was steady, modulated, building a case of unassailable logic.

I cited case law with rhythmic confidence, my movements efficient and devoid of emotion. I was the best version of myself in this room: unreadable, unstoppable.

The problem was, I kept seeing Marcus's face in the marble table's reflection—not the grinning driver, but the vulnerable, desperate man standing by his flower-filled car.

*"I was so terrified of losing the one woman who didn't seem to care about the money, I ruined the very thing I was trying to protect."*

That line. It cut because it sounded like an excuse a man who was used to winning would use. But it also cut because it sounded true. He didn't lie to steal from me; he lied to protect himself. He thought his clever facade was the only thing standing between him and my dismissal.

I closed my rebuttal with a precise, surgical summary, delivering the final sentence that effectively dismantled the opposing argument's foundation. The opposing lawyer flinched. The jury shifted. I had done it.

Walking out during the recess, my colleagues were ecstatic, patting my shoulder and praising my delivery. I barely registered them. I had won the battle in the courtroom, but the bigger, messier war over trust was waiting for me outside, armed with a cell phone and a promise of sincerity.

The hardest part wasn't fighting the other side; it was fighting the small, persistent voice telling me that maybe, just maybe, he hadn't corrupted everything.

# Marcus: Presentation

The adrenaline from the courthouse confrontation had worn off, leaving behind a cold, crushing professional anxiety. I hadn't had a distracted meeting in ten years; my focus was my trademark.

But sitting across the gleaming boardroom table from the representatives of Ocean Drive Resorts, all I could see was Zahra's face, the precise, controlled fury in her eyes as she dismissed my floral apology.

*"Requires no sustained effort,"* she'd said. I needed this deal—the exclusive transportation contract for a

dozen high-end coastal properties—to prove to myself that Marcus Vance, CEO, still functioned.

I was only five minutes into the presentation on projected fleet allocation when my mind fractured. I was supposed to be explaining the predictive routing software, but my internal monologue was shouting: *Is she going to text me back? Will she even answer the phone if I call her?*

I lost the thread entirely. My mouth went dry, and I stared blankly at the slide showing complex optimization algorithms. It was humiliating.

"And... uh... the key to this deployment," I stammered, running a hand over my perfectly knotted tie. "Is ensuring that the... that the reliability of the entire logistical framework... remains above reproach."

I was talking about Zahra, not cars.

Thankfully, Gary—who I often brought to massive pitches for his quiet, stable presence—kicked in with the effortless fluidity of a professional operator covering a glitch.

"What Marcus is emphasizing, Mr. Belltre, is our commitment to real-time driver allocation. By minimizing route variability, we guarantee a $4.2\%$ reduction in estimated client wait times compared to regional competitors. We treat time as a fixed contract." Gary rescued the entire section, using jargon and cold facts to cover my emotional breakdown.

I managed to pull myself together for the Q&A, but the damage was done. When the Ocean Drive team finally left, they shook our hands, their expressions polite but reserved.

"We like the Prime model, Mr. Vance," Beltre said coolly, the lead negotiator. "Your team's analysis is exceptional. However, given the irregularity we noted in your presentation today, we can only agree to a six-month probationary contract. Full exclusive terms will be contingent on performance metrics."

A probationary deal. I hadn't taken a probationary agreement since Prime was two years old. My distraction had cost us a definitive multi-year contract.

I watched the doors click shut, and my composure instantly evaporated. I leaned heavily against the mahogany table, dragging my hands down my face.

"Thank you," I choked out, looking at Gary and my Chief Analyst, Sarah. "You saved my ass. Sarah, that was a masterful cover on the margin projections."

Sarah, never one for sugarcoating, set down her notepad. "You were completely gone, Marcus. That's not like you. You missed three major talking points, and you stared at that algorithm slide for a full minute like it owed you money."

Gary looked at me, his calm gaze heavy with concern. "Are you okay?"

I straightened my tie, trying to conjure the familiar mask of the clever CEO, but the face looking back from the dark boardroom window was just Marcus McNair, ten years old and terrified of the chaos.

"I don't know," I admitted, the most honest thing I had said all week. "I just... Hope I will be."

I grabbed my jacket and walked out, needing the immediate silence of the elevator more than the loyalty of my team. I had six months to fix my professional reputation, and an uncertain amount of time to fix my personal one. And I knew which task was more daunting.

# Zahra: Interrogation

I had won the case, a genuine, high-stakes win that made the firm's partners smile wider than usual. Alicia and I were celebrating at a chic uptown bar—the kind of place where I usually felt obligated to network, but tonight I just wanted to decompress.

I was sipping a celebratory martini, the victory feeling oddly muted by the persistent, simple texts Marcus kept sending. He wasn't following my instructions to stop texting me, but the very effectiveness of his campaign felt like another calculated move. Something in me wouldn't let me block him. Was it because he is a millionaire? Would I even think twice if he weren't who he is? Oh my God, am I shallow? Is his status really making me want to work things out? *Maybe the façade was the right play.* I shook the thought out of my head.

"He sent me a link to an article about the new Ocean Drive deal," I told Alicia, swirling the ice in my glass. "No caption. Just the link. It's either incredibly genuine or intensely tactical."

Alicia laughed, a bright, appreciative sound. "It's both. He's running a controlled experiment on your forgiveness, and you're falling for it. But hey, he's proving he can handle the mundane, which is a good sign."

"Mundane is the opposite of the life he was hiding," I sighed, just as a familiar, barely clothed figure approached our table.

"Zahra! Alicia! What a lovely surprise. You're looking exceptionally successful, darling," Mia cooed, her eyes lingering for just a second too long on the watch Marcus had given me on our third date—a simple, elegant piece I wore because it was classic, not flashy.

"Mia. Congratulations on making it here on time," I replied smoothly. Alicia chuckled under her breath.

Mia, sensing an open wound, signaled the waiter for a glass of champagne and slid into the empty seat, turning her attention to me. "I heard about you two. My deepest sympathies, truly. You seemed so happy playing house with the driver persona. It was adorable."

"The situation is complicated, Mia. It's not about the money," I said, instinctively rising to Marcus's defense.

Mia snorted, a delicate, expensive sound. "Please. That's what they always say. It's absolutely about the money, or rather, the access to the money. Marcus is a headache, girl. He's so wrapped up in being the smartest man in the room, it gets boring."

"Boring? He's the wittiest, most down-to-earth person I've ever met," I argued, feeling a strange obligation to protect the memory of the man who literally stole my heart.

"He talks too much," Mia scoffed, sipping her champagne. "He's always analyzing the market, the logistics, the efficiency of the relationship. He wants to be around you all the time, constantly asking what you think, what you feel. Honestly, it's exhausting. All I wanted was the lifestyle he provided—the travel, the privacy, the access. I didn't want the perpetual deep dive into his soul."

I leaned back, suddenly seeing the reflection of my own past weariness in Mia's jaded confession. *Was* I asking Marcus to perform too much emotional labor?

"But Mia," I pressed, focusing my lawyer's eye on her fundamental lack of loyalty. "If he was such a bore to you, and he gave you the lifestyle you wanted, why did you leave him? You were the one who broke it off, weren't you?"

Mia shrugged, adjusting the massive diamond ring on her finger. The truth, when it came, was delivered with a cold, almost businesslike calculation that left me stunned.

"Because he was only making mid-to-low six figures when we met. He was still building the fleet, not running it. He was focused on the grind, not the glide. It was messy, and honestly, I found someone two years later who was already in his first company making seven figures. Why waste my time on a man who was still in development? I upgraded, boo. It's called intelligent market behavior."

I stared at her, the truth hanging in the air like toxic exhaust. Marcus hadn't lied because he was an arrogant fraud; he had lied because he was terrified of being categorized and rejected by women like Mia—women who saw him only as a number, a financial statement that needed to be upgraded.

The lie, I realized, was his shield against gold-digging, not a weapon against my heart. It was a massive, unforgivable mistake, but the motive was suddenly painfully clear.

The silence that followed Mia's casual cruelty was the loudest sound I'd ever heard. Alicia, God bless her, didn't utter a word, knowing I needed to process the defense strategy myself.

Mia leaned back, completely unaware she had just destroyed the last piece of my self-righteous anger. "He was so desperate for a genuine connection, he just talked and talked about his feelings and his big plans. Honestly, I zoned out half the time. He kept trying to prove he was interesting, but I only cared about the money and sex. It was always about the car, though, so I gave him a chance."

My hands, resting on the cool marble of the table, curled into fists. "So, you rejected him when he was vulnerable and ambitious but not yet rich enough, and now you resent that he found a woman who valued the ambition over the net worth?"

"Resent? No. I just find it funny that he still has to play games to get a woman's attention." Mia stood up, adjusting her tailored jacket. "Seriously, Zahra, let it go. You won your big case. He'll just find another woman who likes the tragic chauffeur story. It's his type."

"So how did it go with the other guy? Or do you just pop up when invited to even the ratio?"

"Don't worry about what I've got going on. As long as that money comes in, nothing else matters."

"Let me guess, he was boring as well?"

"Everything is boring without me, boo. And when you stop looking for whatever it is you are trying to find in these men, and do what you got to do to get to the money, you probably wouldn't be boring and having niggas pretending to be broke."

She walked away, leaving me reeling. Alicia watched her retreating, then turned to me, her eyes filled with a new kind of disgust.

"I thought what he did was arrogance, a man proving he could trick me for sport. But it wasn't. He was genuinely terrified of being used, of being *Mia's type*. He was so scared of being evaluated by his pockets that he chose the ultimate defensive position: playing average."

Alicia picked up her drink. "The betrayal is still there. He didn't trust you. But the motive shifts the analysis. It moves the lie from being a weapon pointed *at* you to a shield he threw up out of fear. And Mia just proved his fear was justified. She literally said she dumped him for a better financial exit."

"And what did I do?" I asked, my voice cracking slightly. "I thought I was too good for him, too 'high-class' for a driver. I reinforced the exact insecurity that led him to lie in the first place." I shook my head, the full circle of the tragedy hitting me. "He was honest with me about his fears, but he just used a ridiculous costume to do it."

"I understand how you feel, but it is okay to have standards. If you don't want to date a driver, then don't date one."

"That's the thing, Al, I wanted him the first time I saw him. He won me over on our first conversation, but I was worried about what my coworkers would think instead of what I felt."

I looked down at my phone. Marcus's last text about the new acquisition fluttered across the screen. He is literally doing everything he said he would do. I was genuinely happy for him and wanted to celebrate our victories together.

*I need to find out if he's ready for something genuine,* I thought, pushing aside my last martini. I want to see if he can stop acting clever and just be the tired man trying to fix his mistake.

I looked at Alicia. "I'm going to reply to. I'm going to follow through. But I need to do it with a new focus: I'm not testing his strategy; I'm observing his sincerity."

# Marcus: The Long Game

The hardest thing I had ever done wasn't surviving my first year in business; it was not being in control of my situation. My entire personality was a rapid-fire succession of calculated charm, but for Zahra, I forced myself into the uncomfortable silence of sincerity. I had built an empire on calculated risk, but the most significant risk I ever faced was this: it was her.

I deleted more texts than I sent. My impulse was to write a three-paragraph analysis on what I did and how I would continue to do what I could to make up for it, but

Gary's words echoed in my ear: *She wants small, consistent effort. No spectacle.*

I followed the instructions exactly. Texts: simple, never asking a question that required more than a one-word answer. The discipline was agonizing. It was like forcing a grand concert pianist only to play the C-major scale, every day, perfectly.

*Wednesday, 7:00 AM: Clear skies here. Hope your day starts well.* (No reply.)

*Friday, 8:15 AM: Just heard a crazy story on the news. Won't bore you. Enjoy the weekend.* (No reply.)

Then, two weeks in, she replied to my article about the ocean drive acquisition. I think she picked up on that trip down the coast we went on, as I was taking notes and pulling over constantly.

*Friday, 10:23 PM: Zahra: That's Great, Marcus!!!*

It was just three words, but it felt like another signed acquisition agreement. A full-sentence reply after weeks of silence. My heart rate kicked up instantly. I fought the urge to call her, to send a follow-up joke, or to order a

Spanish chef to her house. I typed: *Congrats on the big win.* And then I forced myself to wait twenty-four agonizing hours, staring at the muted phone, wondering if my restraint was the right kind of effort or just another form of calculated strategy.

I went two more weeks, focused entirely on consistency. I kept my texts simple. The ritual of the coffee drop was my new penance. I would drive a clean, top-of-the-line vehicle to her office building—the exact vehicle I use for our VIP clients—and walk into the lobby.

I'd buy her favorite cold brew at the cafe, feeling the heat of my own face, knowing I was a massive, visible spectacle in my tailored suit jacket and tie-less shirt. I would then walk to the security desk and hand the cup and a small, folded card to the guard. The card carried my name, title, and company: *Marcus Vance, CEO, Prime Executive Transportation.*

I did that three times. The first time, one of the guards gave me a suspicious look that mirrored every gold-digger I'd ever dated. The second time, she recognized me and merely raised an eyebrow. The third time, she just nodded, accepting my everyday devotion as a new, remarkable part of the lobby's routine. It was the hardest thing I'd ever done: acting without expectation of reward, simply for the sake of the effort.

On the fifth week, I took a rare day off. Instead of fishing, I drove to the basketball court where Gary, Lee, and I used to play as kids. It was a run-down park, nothing fancy. The chain net was snapped, the lines were faded, and the backboard was a warped relic of my youth.

I sat on the cracked bench, feeling a sense of quiet nostalgia. I took a picture of the worn, peeling backboard and sent it to Zahra.

*Text: This is where I learned how to lose a game gracefully. It's taken me twenty years to apply the lesson.*

Fifteen minutes later, my phone buzzed. My hands actually shook as I opened the text.

*Zahra: The court looks like it needs some work done..*

*Me: I know a guy who owns a transportation company. Maybe he can figure out something for a rebuild.*

*Zahra: That guy should focus less on logistics and more on simple honesty. And if he's free soon, I'd like to see the backboard in person.*

I closed my eyes, the victory a slow, deep breath, entirely devoid of the thrill of a business conquest. It was better. I had earned the right to try again, not with a million-dollar gesture, but with four weeks of silent, consistent truth.

# Marcus: The Do Over

The text was my final authorization. *If he's free soon, I'd like to see the backboard in person.*

I didn't arrive with flowers or a freshly detailed sedan. I came to the court in a battered pickup truck borrowed from my Head of Maintenance, wearing worn jeans and a faded, paint-splattered Prime company shirt—the one I'd worn ten years ago when I was still doing the grunt work. I called Gary and Lee.

"I need help rebuilding a basketball court. No jokes, Lee. Pure manual labor. We can do most of the grunt work ourselves, but let's call in a few favors as well."

They met me there, the three of us under the glare of industrial floodlights I had borrowed from a construction site that a client owned.

We spent the next several weeks stripping the decaying asphalt, patching the deep cracks in the foundation, and finally, using my old high school paint stencils, laying down crisp new boundary lines. It was honest, back-breaking work—sweat, grit, and silence, broken only by the steady scrape of the tools.

I used my wealth not to buy something, but to fund a service project with a single audience. I paid for the highest quality, professional-grade materials, but I applied them myself, by hand, with the only two people who knew the real story of Marcus Vance.

Word started to get around, and more people began to show up every day. Each of them was bringing their own talents and connections to the project. It felt good to come back to the old neighborhood and do something for the community that shaped my future.

I was rebuilding a memory. Every swing of the sledgehammer against the old backboard was a blow against my own arrogance. Every time I ran the paint roller over the new court lines, I was etching a new commitment into the asphalt.

A news crew pulled up near the end of the project to report on the court's restoration. "Whose idea was this?" a reporter asked the group.

Everyone looked around, and their eyes settled on me. "It's mine," I said loud and proud.

"Do you mind if we do an interview?" Usually, I would decline any press, but I didn't want to hide anything else about me or my past.

"Sure, let's do it."

"Good morning. I am Cierra with QC news, and behind me is the beautiful restoration project of this long-forgotten basketball court. And with me, I have the project's organizer. Can you tell us who you are and what inspired you to do this?"

"I am Marcus Vance, CEO of Prime Executive Transportation. I grew up here. Back when being part of a community meant something, before my mother was killed down the street by a drunk driver, before resources were reallocated to other districts and left us to fend for ourselves."

"Oh my… You are MacMac."

"Now that is a name that I have not heard in decades. Yes, my last name was McNair before it was changed. I was ashamed of the burden that name held, but it is a part of me, just like this basketball court. I hope this will mark the start of a revival of this community and the surrounding area. Remember, if you have to go, go with Prime." I ended with my company tagline.

"Yes, we will, and thank you for your story. Well, there you have it, hope and hoops in this neighborhood that was in need of a do-over. Hopefully, this will inspire others to act. I am Cierra with QC News. Goodbye, and take care."

When I turned around, everyone was staring at me. I could feel the emotions welling up inside me. Everyone started to clap and cheer for what we accomplished and for the realization of who I was, and what my mother meant to the community. It felt good.

Just before sunset, with the paint drying on the fresh lines, I stood back, covered in dust and sweat, a profound, primal exhaustion settling in my bones. Lee and Gary had left, leaving me alone. I heard a car pull up across the court. I turned to see, and there she was. Zahra...

# Zahra: The Closing Arguments

Anticipation was killing me. He texted me this morning and sent me the park's address. Usually, I am good at picking out something to wear, but this time, I felt so indecisive.

The sun was setting when I pulled up to the park in my own reliable, slightly older sedan. I expected the park, but I didn't expect the sight before me: the court was transformed.

It was immaculate. The asphalt was smooth and fresh—ready for its first full court game. The peeling backboard was gone, replaced by a gleaming, official-looking new hoop. The lines—the precise, geometric boundaries I appreciated in my profession—were a sharp, undeniable white against the blacktop. It wasn't just the court. The landscaping was amazing. Colorful flowers were around the gates, and the smell of gardenia bushes hung over them like a shield.

And there was Marcus. Not in a suit, not leaning against a luxury car, but sitting on the ground next to a can of paint thinner, his face streaked with dirt, his company shirt clinging to his sweat-soaked back.

He looked spent, genuine, and handsome. The man was exhausted, his physical labor a stark contrast to his usual mental gymnastics. I walked onto the court, my heels clicking softly on the new surface.

"This is very impressive. I am so proud of you, Marcus," I said, my voice steady, but my heart pounding.

He slowly rose, his movements stiff, favoring his left knee slightly. "I had to find a way to use the resources for something meaningful. This place, this court, is the last non-negotiable truth of who I am. It's where I learned that effort matters more than talent sometimes. It's where I was just... Marcus."

"It's beautiful," I whispered, walking to the center court line. "But you know I wasn't talking about the court."

"I know." He stepped toward me, stopping outside the half-court line, a respectable distance. "The lie was a crack in the foundation. I used my time, my hands, and the help of the only two people who ever called me out on my nonsense to patch it. It's not perfect, but it's stable now. And I guarantee it's ready for whatever. I am ready for you, no more cracks, Z."

I looked at the new backboard, then at the man standing opposite me. I saw not the brilliant liar, but the exhausted man who had spent the last several weeks on his knees, proving his worth with labor, not talk. This was the vulnerable truth I had been waiting for.

"You said you learned to lose gracefully here," I said, finally stepping over the line toward him. "I don't want you to lose, Marcus. I want you to be honest with yourself and with me, Marcus."

I reached out, gently touching the dirt smudge on his cheek. "I accept the closing argument. And I'm willing to start rebuilding, one day at a time, on this new foundation."

Marcus didn't smile his usual charming grin. His expression was pure relief, a silent exhale of weeks of held-in tension. He closed the remaining distance, his arms wrapping around me in a hug that was less about passion and more about solid, hard-won certainty. He had spent weeks trying to win a case, and he had finally earned my heart, the right way.

# Alicia: The Unofficial Friends Merger

Zahra had given me one instruction: *Vet the friends. I need to know the entire support structure isn't built on another witty deception.*

So, here I was, sipping a dangerously strong martini in a dimly lit, slightly greasy sports bar—a place smelling faintly of spilled beer and old neon—waiting for the men who had been complicit in this facade.

Marcus wasn't there; this was a friends-only summit. Gary and Lee arrived exactly five minutes after I did. Gary, quiet and sharp, looked like a respectable accountant who secretly read philosophy. Lee, the goofball, looked like he was auditioning for a Making the Band type show. He was talking animatedly about a fishing lure as they slid into the booth.

"Alicia. I'm Lee, and this is Gary, the voice of reason and the man who can bench-press a mid-sized sedan," Lee announced, immediately grabbing the conversational reins. "Pleasure to meet the woman who runs a PR firm but couldn't spin Marcus's little chauffeur side-gig."

"It's not a chauffeur side-gig when he owns the chauffeurs, Lee. It's method acting, and I know you all are crazy," I countered, not breaking eye contact. "And my job is truth management. You two were the co-conspirators in the willful misrepresentation of my best friend's boyfriend. Explain yourselves."

Gary laughed, a surprisingly deep, non-judgmental sound. "We tried to tell him, Alicia. Marcus is cleverness incarnate. You tell him he needs to be honest, and he thinks that means being honest about the lie, not just honest without the lie. He didn't want the money to cloud her judgment."

"It was pure performance art!" Lee insisted, waving his hand wildly, nearly knocking over my martini. "He literally said he had to win her over as the driver, or the whole thing was invalidated. We were advising him on how to maintain the character arc! I told him he needed a tragic backstory. Maybe a sick goldfish."

"He had a legitimate point, actually," Gary interjected, setting down his beer carefully. "He's sick of the money being the filter. He wanted a clean slate. She just happened to be the woman who gave it to him, even if it meant being rejected for not meeting your imaginary financial minimum."

I stared at them, absorbing the dynamic. Gary was Marcus's conscience—the steady base. Lee was his id—the hilarious, chaotic relief. They were exactly who Marcus needed, and they clearly adored him. The anger, which had been a low, consistent hum, finally dissipated. They weren't corporate villains; they were just two men trying to keep their overly clever friend from self-sabotaging.

"I suppose you're right," I conceded, picking up my martini. "The sheer effort he put into the lie was almost commendable. He used his entire company to play the part of a mere employee. That takes dedication."

Lee beamed. "See? It's peak performance! And he did the grand gesture! The court, right? I told him to buy an island, but the court was way less embarrassing. Gary said he just needed to use his hands for once."

I took a slow sip. "The court was perfect. It was authentic. But Lee," I leaned in, my voice dropping to a serious, lawyerly whisper. "If you ever mention Prime Executive Transport's CEO to a stranger again, I will buy every single fishing lure you own, and send them, one by one, to Zahra's office, marked 'Confidential Business Information.'"

Lee swallowed hard, his goofy smile dissolving into genuine fear. "Duly noted, Ms. Hayes's Counsel. Complete silence on the fleet status. Understood."

I smiled. "Good. Now, tell me everything about this Mia character. I need to know who I'm dealing with in future social situations."

# Epilogue: Six Months Later

**Marcus**

Six months. That's how long we'd been cohabiting in my penthouse, well, it feels like it, how much she is over here. My glass cage is now gently populated with Zahra's decorations. Her stacks of law briefs, her comfortable, worn yoga mats, and a ridiculous vintage reading lamp that completely ruined the living room's minimalist aesthetic. And I loved every single disruptive element of it.

The most significant change in my life was her. The effort I used to put into maintaining the "driver" persona is now invested in building out the non-profit she cares about—the legal aid clinic for domestic violence victims. My logistics team handles their transport schedules at no cost. My wealth, for the first time, feels like a simple utility, a shovel used to dig foundations for things that actually matter to her.

I walked out onto the balcony, coffee in hand. Zahra was already up, sitting outside in a massive cashmere sweater, reviewing depositions. She still woke up in fight-or-flight mode, but she wasn't scared of me anymore.

"Good morning, Counselor," I said, leaning down to kiss the top of her head.

"Morning. I need to figure out the fastest route to the D.C. office next Tuesday. Think you can handle the logistics?" she teased, her eyes sparkling.

"I know a guy," I replied, taking a sip of coffee. "He knows the only non-stop private route takes precisely four hours and forty-two minutes, but he's already blocked out the extra hour for traffic. Consider it handled."

The money was now just a piece of shared information, like our opposing work schedules or our tax file. There were still awkward moments, like when I had to remind her that yes, we absolutely did own the entire floor, and no, she didn't have to keep closing the door to the unused gym. But the truth was, she had anchored me. She brought the honesty I needed, and I brought the stability she craved.

Lee still insisted I bought her too many expensive "apology gifts," but Gary had it right: *The best gesture you can make is showing up.* And I was here. Sweaty, honest, and utterly free of the driver's cap.

## Zahra

It's astonishing how quickly a massive, life-altering truth can become a domestic reality. Marcus Vance, the man who owns the entire transport infrastructure of this city, snores slightly and insists on ordering the same French-roast coffee blend every single day. The lie is dead, and the man who remains is everything I fell for—the precision, the quiet competence, the intense focus—only now, it's all turned towards me as often as it's turned towards Prime.

The wealth used to feel like a massive, dense barrier, a wall Marcus erected to test my worth. Now, it feels like shared scaffolding. When I talk about my frustrations with pro bono work, he doesn't just listen; he quietly figures out the logistics to solve the structural problems I encounter. He's the CEO who has the competence to fix my small, necessary corner of the world.

I looked down at my phone, pulling up a photo from last Saturday. It was Lee, Gary, and Alicia, all crammed onto Lee's ancient, barely floating fishing boat on Lake Travis.

Alicia was wearing a ridiculously oversized sunhat and a look of profound skepticism, holding a fishing rod as if it were a complex litigation exhibit. Lee was gesturing wildly, explaining the spiritual connection between the lure and the trout's destiny.

*"He says it's 'quiet competence,' but I call it 'meditative silence with the occasional beer,'"* Alicia had texted me afterward.

That trip was everything. Alicia, the master of PR performance, spent the entire day fighting Lee, the master of pure, unfiltered chaos. I later learned Lee was trying to teach Alicia how to tie a "goofball knot," which is apparently a triple granny knot that fails 80% of the time. Alicia was threatening to file a class-action suit against him for gross negligence.

Gary, of course, spent the entire day quietly baiting Alicia's hook and then whispering the correct knot technique to her twenty minutes later. They were the perfect calibration for us: Lee and Alicia were the chaotic, witty extremes; Gary and Marcus were the steady, honest constants.

I learned two great lessons. First, I wasn't scared of dating a driver; I was scared of dating a liar, and the fact that Marcus thought he had to lie was the real heart of the problem. Second, the man I fell in love with wasn't the driver or the CEO; he was a hybrid—the man obsessed with making things run perfectly. Now, he's focused on making *us* run perfectly.

I looked up from my brief as Marcus came over, putting his heavy, competent hand on my shoulder. I leaned into his touch, feeling the simple, solid reality of him.

"You won't be able to stay in the city this weekend, will you?" I asked, anticipating the chaos of a major corporate merger he was managing.

"I will," he replied, his voice firm. "I finished the model last night. I've scheduled the long meetings for Friday and delegated oversight of the entire weekend to my Head of Operations. I made a promise to the woman I love that I'd be present, and I'm damn good at keeping promises. Consider it a non-negotiable term of our merger."

I looked up at him, smiling. "Duly noted, Counselor." I stood up, kissing him deeply, tasting the french roast and the steady, clean truth of him. The past was over. The game had ended. The only thing left was us.

# Bonus Content

*"Yes, we will, and thank you for your story. Well, there you have it, hope and hoops in this neighborhood that was in need of a do-over. Hopefully, this will inspire others to act. I am Cierra with QC News. Goodbye, and take care."*

In a basement across town, three men were standing watching the news in a pool hall. Their eyes were glued to the television.

"Isn't that the dude's son that killed your dad?" One of them said. Everyone turned and looked at the man as he called his shot.

"Eight ball in the corner," he hit the cue ball with a spin that made the ball bounce off the rail when it made contact with the eight ball. The eight ball rolled and went into the corner pocket just. "Let's take a ride."

# Marketing and Engagement

*Out of the Window is Available on Amazon*

## About the Author

I'm T.J. Polk, and I craft immersive fiction where epic
fantasy collides with heart-pounding thriller intensity.
My journey began in Fort Polk, Louisiana, fueled by
comics and a deep curiosity that led me through military
service, global travel, and the discovery of my family.
After making profound personal sacrifices and retiring
from the Army, writing became my sanctuary. Now based
in Georgia, and author of *"Out of the Window,"* I invite
you into dark, intriguing worlds, hoping you enjoy
reading my stories as much as I enjoyed writing them.